MY WEEK WITH THE BAD BOY

MY WEEK, #1

BROOKE CUMBERLAND
& LYRA PARISH

My Week with the Bad Boy

WITH THE Bad Boy

BROOKE CUMBERLAND
AND LYRA PARISH

"Not a day goes by that I don't think of you.
I'm always asking why this crazy world had to lose
such a ray of light we never knew.
Gone too soon…"

-Gone Too Soon,
Daughtry

CHAPTER ONE

VADA

THE PLANE RATTLES and shakes as it prepares to make its landing. Cringing, I steady myself on the armrest, but when I place my hand down, it touches the guy sitting next to me.

"Oh, shit. Sorry." I jerk my hand back and wrap my arms around my body.

"It's okay. Take it," the older gentleman offers. I'm not afraid of flying, but I don't exactly love it either. Especially when it feels like we're about to fly straight into the ground.

"Are you sure?" I ask although he's already removed his arm. He nods, and I graciously wrap my fingers around it and squeeze. "Thank you."

We finally land, and once we deplane, I grab my carry-on and head for the baggage claim. I can already feel the heat and am completely overdressed in my black leggings, winter boots, and thick scarf. South Carolina feels like a sauna, and I can almost taste the heat and humidity.

I hail a taxi and inform the driver where I'm going. It's at

1

least another two hours before we'll arrive at the house, but it'll be worth it. Quiet, solitary, peace. Just what I need to finish my novel. As soon as I open the car door, the scent of the ocean blows in the air. It smells like heaven.

"Thank you," I tell the driver when he pulls my luggage out of the trunk.

"You definitely aren't from around here, huh?" he comments, taking in my appearance and bad wardrobe choice. I furrow my brows, wondering if that's meant as a bad thing. "You have a midwestern accent." He confirms his suspicions.

"Oh, yes. Chicago," I tell him. "I'm definitely not in the city anymore." I laugh, grabbing for my wallet. Chicago has been home to me for years, but it's loud, attracts tourists all year round, and neighbors are so close, you can hear them pee. I can only drown out the noise for so long before it drives me insane which led me to booking an Airbnb for a week.

"It's a whole different world out here," he tells me.

I hand him the money with a smile. "That's what I'm hoping for."

As the taxi drives away, I grab my luggage and take in the scenery. It's stunning. The Airbnb I rented is a small guest-house with a garden view. The pictures were amazing, so I'm looking forward to staying in this little peaceful sanctuary for the next week.

Walking up the sidewalk to the main house, I notice a cute porch swing on the patio and some planters along the porch steps. The owner seemed very charming and kind by the pictures, description, and detailed information he wrote for the listing. Everything screams southern. I like it. In fact, I like it a lot.

I ring the bell, and when the door opens wide, my eyes scan up and down the man's body, and I'm shocked to see he's completely shirtless. He's wearing low-cut jeans that ride effortlessly on his hips.

He's maybe a couple years older than me. Dark hair is tousled across his forehead, piercings in his ears, facial hair grazes his hard jawline, and rock-hard abs line his stomach. I swallow as my eyes roam down to the deep V that disappears into his low-cut jeans. He's rugged and manly and definitely *not* what I expected to answer the door. He's the epitome of a bad boy character I'd write about in one of my romance novels, and I'm not sure if that's a good or bad thing.

It's official. I'm undeniably not in Chicago anymore.

"Can I help you or do you plan to stand here and stare at me all evening?" he asks in a faint southern accent; his words take me completely off guard.

I snap my eyes back up and watch him as he studies my features. "That's a rather crass assumption."

"Not an assumption, ma'am."

"Don't call me ma'am. My name is Vada Collins. I rented the guesthouse," I explain, tilting my chin toward the back yard.

"Vada? Hm." He strokes his fingers along his scruff as he narrows his eyes at me.

"What?"

"I wouldn't have pegged you for a Vada. In fact, I read your name as *Vat*-ah."

"Yeah, that's happened all my life." I sigh. "Thanks, Mom and Dad," I mutter to myself, but he chuckles anyway.

"It's cute."

3

I narrow my eyes at him, annoyed that he just called my name *cute*.

"Don't call my name that. I'm not an eight-year-old girl."

"Fuck. You're feisty, aren't you? I like that in a woman." He winks, and it sends a shiver down my spine. What the hell is happening?

"Are you for real?" I ask.

"As real as my twenty-inch cock. Care to come in and see it?" He takes a step to the side and sweeps his arm from one side to the other, motioning for me to come in.

"Excuse me?" I nearly choke on my tongue and take a step back as I envision him pulling down his pants and whipping out his anaconda. "Are you insane or something?"

"Inviting you inside is what we folks down here call southern hospitality, sweetheart." He flashes me one of those smirks I'd write about in my novels where the girl's panties instantly combust, and although this man is sex on a stick, I'm not falling for it.

"I do not want to come inside and see your python-sized cock, okay? Just give me the keys, and I'll find my way around."

He starts laughing. *Laughing*. The asshole.

"Sweetheart, I wasn't talking about my python-sized cock —although you aren't wrong on how big it is—but I was literally talking about my rooster, Henry."

Wait. *What*?

"You have a rooster?" My brows rise, and I can feel my cheeks starting to heat. I've just made a complete ass out of myself, and it's all his fault.

"That's what I said. He likes to wander around the back-

4

yard, so don't get freaked if you see him around the guesthouse."

I groan, closing my eyes to release the added stress. "Great, I'll be sure to watch for him." I hold my palm out flat in front of me. "The keys? Can I have them please?"

His hand reaches for his pocket but then stops. "Not so fast. I need to go over the rules and stipulations first."

"I read all of the rules online when I booked the place. I know what your *stipulations* are. I'm tired, I smell like airplane, and I just want to take a hot shower," I explain, but he ignores me.

"Follow me," he calls out, walking into the house and leaving me both confused and speechless on the porch.

I step inside with my rolling suitcase and follow behind him. The wheels from my luggage rattle against the hardwood floor, and before I can fix it, he turns around, grabs my suitcase, and carries it on his shoulder.

"Are you going to tell me your name?" I ask, realizing I only know him by his name on the Airbnb site—E. Rochester. Sounds made up now that I see him in the flesh. He looks more like a Mr. Robinson. Probably seduces young women and takes their youth and then bails. Or maybe the E stands for egotistical.

"No. Are you going to tell me your favorite position?"

"What?" I screech, certain I heard him wrong.

"Of baseball," he clarifies, looking over his other shoulder at me, sporting an infamous panty-melting smirk.

"I don't—"

"It feels like you're hoarding baseballs or bowling balls in here. Shit."

I narrow my brows, annoyed he continues to make sexual comments about normal things while knowing exactly what he's doing. And I'm giving him just the reaction he's hoping for.

Dammit.

"It's books actually," I correct him. "I'm a writer."

"A writer? Really?" He sets the luggage down in the middle of the kitchen that looks like it came straight from a *Country Living* magazine. "I wouldn't have pegged you as a writer either."

"What does that mean?" I ask, folding my arms over my chest defensively. I've known this guy for all of five minutes, and already he's labeling and pissing me off.

"You look like a basic girl. I assumed you were a dancer or something. Maybe a gymnast. Or hell, even a model."

I'm not sure what the hell he's talking about, but I'm pretty certain that kind of sounded like a compliment?

"What's a basic girl?"

"You know, hair up in one of those ironic messy buns that probably took you at least ten minutes to get *just right*. You're wearing tight, black leggings with gray Ugg boots, and one of those scarfs that's more for fashion than it is useful." He shrugs, unapologetically. "All you're missing is a Starbucks Pumpkin Spice Latte in your hand and a pair of Gucci sunglasses."

"And that makes me a basic girl?"

"That's right, sweetheart."

I point a finger in the air at him. "Don't call me sweetheart," I tell him, annoyed. "And is that what they consider southern hospitality down here because, if so, I gotta say—not impressed."

He laughs again, and it actually sounds real. "Just laying out the facts."

"Well, I mean, if that's what we do around here with someone you literally met minutes ago, I'd say it's my turn."

"Go for it. Give me your best." He crosses his muscular arms over his broad chest, and it takes me a moment to remind myself to stop looking at his incredible body. Getting a better view of him in the light, I see a layer of sweat or water covering his chest and torso. Either he was working out or just got out of the shower. But who the hell works out in jeans, especially in this gross humidity?

"Well, for starters, you answer the door shirtless. You have this whole edgy, bad boy look going on, which is probably because you think you're God's gift to women. Probably in a band and are used to sleeping with groupies every weekend. You flash that smirk around as if you know it gets you whatever you want, which if I were anything *like* a basic girl, I would fall head over heels for. You strut your body off as if it's the only way to grab my attention in hopes I'll just start stripping off all my clothes. Your hands look rugged and have calluses, so aside from playing in a band on Friday and Saturday nights, you work with your hands. A mechanic or builder, maybe."

He studies me as I continue to ramble, looking over his physique and handing out every stereotype he matches. If he wants to judge me based on five seconds of meeting me, then I have no choice but to do the same.

"So, how close am I?" I ask, feeling confident with my assumptions.

He purses his lips and nods. "I'm impressed."

"Well, I do have a knack for reading people. It's what makes me a great writer."

"Is that so?" He arches a brow, and I nod confidently. "Well, I'm sorry to disappoint you, sweetheart, but you couldn't be further from the truth," he says, matter-of-factly. "However," he continues in a low seductive tone, "you are right about one thing."

I roll my eyes and groan. "What's that, Casanova?"

"I was hoping you'd start stripping off all your clothes."

"You're so vain," I hiss at him. "I would never—"

"You're wearing six layers of clothing in ninety-degree weather," he cuts me off. "Stripping off your clothes is to make sure you don't pass out from a heatstroke on my newly remodeled kitchen floor."

I release a long-exaggerated breath, seriously over his sexual remarks and condescending attitude.

"If this is what southern men are like, count me out."

"Oh, I wouldn't worry about that. Your basic girl snark and sarcasm will scare them off for you."

I bite my tongue to keep from cursing him out. I don't have the energy to deal with this egotistical asshole.

"Can we just skip the rules and whatever else for now, and just give me the damn key, please? I've been traveling all day, I'm exhausted, and I need to wash the travel stench off me."

"I wasn't going to say anything but—"

"Can you just *please* stop being a dick for one minute?" I pinch my eyes shut and inhale deeply.

He raises his brows and then reaches into his pocket, revealing the keychain with a single key hanging from it. "Your wish is my command." He holds it out, and I quickly grab it before he can pull it away.

"Thank you," I say, firmly. He opens the back door for me and points me in the direction of the guesthouse.

He stays silent as I grab my suitcase and roll it behind me down the porch steps. The walkway to the guesthouse is lined with gorgeous flowers and bushes that I hadn't expected, especially after meeting the owner—who, by the way, I still didn't get his name.

I spin around, determined to make him tell me, but when I do, a swarm of bugs start biting the shit out of me.

"Oh my God!" I wave my hands around frantically, spinning and trying to get away. I scream, hoping he'll help me or at least get me out of here, but all I hear from his direction is laughter.

"What the fuck?" I shout, thrashing my arms around, trying to dodge them.

"If you had let me finish, I would've told you that your perfume was too strong. It attracts the mosquitoes. But so does travel body odor and sweat."

"You asshole," I mutter, knowing he'll hear me anyway.

"Tried to warn ya," he says casually, and when I look up at him, he's leaning against the doorway with his arms crossed like the smug asshole he is.

CHAPTER TWO

ETHAN

AFTER A LONG DAY OF WORK, I'm ready to call it a night. Windows paint the walls of the third-story tower room in my house that I use as a workspace. Although it's my favorite room, it gets hot as hell. Hotter than the rest of the house, especially in Charleston during the summer. But it's the only place I find inspiration anymore, so I work through it.

I jump in the shower and clean off the aftermath. This time of year, I usually wait for it to cool off and work in the evenings and night, but my schedule's jam packed between working and showings, that I need to squeeze it in when I can. Just as I'm putting on a pair of jeans, I hear doors slam outside, and when I peek out the window, I see a woman and a taxi driver talking on the sidewalk. Assuming it's my tenant for the week, I rush downstairs before putting on a shirt.

The moment she eyes me, I can read the judgment all over her face. I decide this can go two ways: I can dazzle her with my southern charm and prove she's wrong about me, or

I can have some fun and mess with this unmistakable city girl.

I choose the latter.

She's attractive in an obvious way. Pretty face, long, lean legs, chocolate-brown hair—the type of girl who could get by on her looks alone. When I open the door and see her standing on my front porch, I notice that her eyes are a sparkling green, or perhaps that's just how they look when she's annoyed. Either way, she's got that girl-next-door mixed with a *Sex and the City* vibe. Innocent and classy, but could probably break me in more ways than one. Her sass proves that immediately.

Staring at me, her eyes continue to roam up and down my body. I smirk, knowing she's checking me out just as I was her. Though as soon as I speak, her attitude shifts and gives out a look of disgust. I find it humorous, really, because I know her type—uppity and snobbish. She pretends to be unaffected by me and then offended when I ask if she plans to stare at me all night.

And when she answers me, in that tone and scowl, I know I'm completely right about her.

The next morning, I wake up with Wilma's ass in my face. She's a feisty feline who doesn't give two shits about personal space or boundaries and wiggles her way under the covers until she's comfortable. She's purring softly, which means she's still sleeping, but that doesn't stop me from pushing her away.

"Nice work, Wilma," I groan. "Woke me up before my alarm, so I'll actually have time to make coffee this morning."

She stretches and meows before rolling onto her back and waits for me to pet her. I give in and then get dressed before I get too comfortable and fall back asleep.

"C'mon, Wilma. Let's get breakfast."

I slip on my jeans before heading downstairs. The sun is rising over the water and streaks of reds and oranges are shining through the bay windows. It's gorgeous. My favorite part of the day actually, but since I've been working more than usual lately, I'm usually getting up before the sunrise.

After refilling Wilma's food and water, I fill the coffee maker and pull out my mug. Just as I'm digging in the fridge for some creamer, a knock at the back door startles me.

"Shit," I curse when I see it's Vada. She looks like she literally just rolled out of bed with messy hair and sleepy eyes. It's actually kind of cute.

"You scared the living shit out of me," I tell her once I open the door. "What are you doing up so early?"

"Sorry," she apologizes, pulling her robe tighter around her waist. "I work best in the morning and was trying to get a head start, but...there's no coffee maker."

"And here I thought you were coming for another viewing." I cross my arms over my chest, emphasizing my biceps.

"Funny." She rolls her eyes, swallowing back a groan that tells me she's not in the mood for any games. "After letting me get swarmed with mosquitos, the least you could do is let me have some coffee," she tells me matter-of-factly.

I grin, leaning against the door. "Well...that's not the *least* I could do..."

"Oh, fuck it. I'll get dressed and go into town for coffee."

She turns, but before she can walk away, I step forward and grab her arm.

"Oh, come on." I chuckle, finding everything about her amusing. "You don't need to go into town scaring the locals with your raccoon eyes and rat's nest. I made coffee."

She studies me for a moment, staying silent. Her eyes roam down to where my fingers are gripped around her wrist. I remove them and wait for her to say something. Her breath hitches and I wonder if it's because our bodies are so close — we're nearly chest to chest — or if it's from the loss of my touch. Either way, it doesn't go unnoticed.

"Fine," she grits between her teeth. "Only because I'm desperate."

I cough to cover up a smile as I widen the door and wave her inside.

Once she steps in, I shut the door behind her and point a finger to the cupboard near the fridge. "Coffee mugs are in there."

"Thank you." She walks over and reaches inside for one of my mugs, wrapping her fingers securely around it and studies it. "These are spectacular. Where did you find them?" She brushes her fingers across the markings and smooth surface. Tilting it over, she reads the bottom. "Paris?"

Clearing my throat, I adjust myself, so we're parallel from each other. I lean up against the island and watch as she admires the mug. "There's a shop in town that sells them. I probably have a dozen or so."

"Wow…I'm impressed."

I arch a brow and smile. "With the mug or that I actually own a piece like that?"

She grins. "Both."

The coffee maker beeps, signaling it's finished brewing. She pours herself a cup, reaches for the creamer in the fridge, and sits down at the breakfast bar. I follow suit, filling my own mug and then sit down on the stool across from her.

We study each other as she blows carefully in her mug, and before either of us speak up, Wilma makes herself known and rubs up against Vada's dangling legs.

"Oh, hello," she coos in a soft, sweet voice. "And who are you?" Wilma reaches up and paws at her, begging for attention as usual.

"That's Wilma," I tell her. She brings the mug to her lips and takes a small sip as I continue. "She's the only pussy allowed in my bed, so don't get any ideas."

Before I can react, hot coffee spews from her mouth and lands on my bare chest and face.

"Oh my God!" She covers her mouth and laughs. "Why would you say something like that?"

"Wasn't it obvious? To get your hot saliva all over me."

She tilts her head and narrows her eyes. "Do you ever stop?"

I purse my lips as if I'm truly contemplating her question. "Nah. I live for reactions like yours."

"For some reason, I don't doubt that for one second." She scowls, reaching for the paper towels on the counter and handing them to me.

"Aren't you going to at least clean me up? I mean, it was your fault and all."

Rolling her eyes, she takes the roll out of my hand and

smacks me in the head with it. "Actually, you brought that on all by yourself. So nice try, Casanova."

After cleaning up the coffee mess, I sit back and watch as she pours herself another cup. "So what's with this term of endearment, Casanova? Does that mean you want to be seduced and bedded or you actually think I'm *that* kind of guy?"

"*Seduced and bedded*?" She laughs, walking back to the stool with her mug of hot coffee. I eye it, making sure she doesn't spontaneously trip and dump the entire thing on me.

"You sound like you've been reading historical romance or something."

"Not since I was fifteen and stealing the novels off my grandmother's bookshelf."

"You read romance novels when you were a teenager?"

"Only in hopes it came with pictures," I shamelessly admit, mocking the way she's throwing jabs at me. "That was before online porn, so I had to do what I had to do." I shrug, and she bursts out in laughter. I like the sound—a lot, actually. Although she's a bit uptight, I enjoy watching her laugh. The wrinkles in her face, the freckles that move along her cheeks, and the sweet sound that releases from her throat. It's adorable.

Once she controls her laughter, she straightens her posture and purses her lips. "And for the record, it's not a term of endearment."

I'm quick to press my palm flat against my chest, showing defeat. "Why must you break my heart?"

Her head falls back with laughter, louder than before and I can tell it's genuine. She's warming up to me even if she pretends she doesn't like me.

"As much as I'm enjoying this little early morning chat with you, I have to get back to my laptop and start writing. Otherwise, this entire trip will be a bust, and I'll never be able to write again."

"You just got here, so don't put too much pressure on yourself."

"Says the person who doesn't write." She rolls her eyes as she stands up and takes the mug with her. "There's no such thing as too much pressure. It's a part of the lifestyle. You're either writing, or you're not writing. There's no in-between."

"Fair enough." I shrug.

"Thanks again for the coffee." She holds up the mug in a peace-offering salute. "I'll be sure to bring it back in one piece."

"That's not even funny," I say seriously, pointing a finger at her. "I saw the way you stumbled to the guesthouse last night, so I'm not sure how trustworthy your word is."

She gasps, and her jaw drops in mock laughter. "I was nearly killed by a swarm of bugs while you just stood there and laughed!"

"I didn't laugh," I defend. "But it was pretty funny considering you were in the middle of scolding me."

She sighs and rolls her eyes, giving up the fight. Although we'd just met, I can actually read her quite well. She's snarky and quick-witted, just like me, except she knows when to give up. Me—not so much.

She opens the door, and just before stepping out, looks over her shoulder and smirks. "Have a good day, Casanova."

CHAPTER THREE

VADA

HE KISSES HER SOFTLY, plucking his thumb along her lower lip, and when she releases a hungry, desperate moan, he slides his tongue in deeper. Helena arches her back, and Jordan wraps his arms around her waist, pressing her body tighter against his. She feels his growing erection against her flesh and can no longer resist the temptation to touch him. She's been waiting years for this moment...

Writing sex scenes is the hardest part of the writing process for me. Even though I usually have great feedback from my agent, it takes twice as long to write compared to other scenes. It doesn't help that I haven't been inspired due to my own pathetic love life.

Leaning back in my chair, I stretch my arms over my head and crack my neck from side to side. I can only write for a few hours at a time before I need to get up and walk around. I'm usually alternating between writing and social media, but I vowed to take a social media break while I'm on my mini writing retreat.

Casanova had mentioned downtown Charleston and all the quaint shops that line the street. Chicago is covered in shops and malls, but there's just something about a new city that intrigues me. I close my laptop and decide a short break wouldn't hurt. Hell, it might inspire me for the first time in weeks.

After showering and getting dressed, I stop by the main house to ask for suggestions on where I should go, but he's not home. He must've left for work or something, so I schedule an Uber to take me downtown.

"Thank you," I tell the driver after he drops me off on the corner of King and Meeting Street by Marion Square Park. He suggested this area once I told him I wasn't exactly sure where I wanted to go, and I'm happy to see he didn't let me down. I can already tell it's what I was needing.

"Enjoy yourself," he tells me with a smile before I shut the door behind me.

Shops are lined up and down both sides of King Street. The sun is shining brightly above, people are chatting as they walk past, and a high energy is in the air.

Usually being around a lot of people gives me anxiety, but today I plan to embrace it. Chicago's always crowded with tourists sight-seeing and locals walking to work, which is why I usually stay isolated in my shoebox apartment. But not here. I want to enjoy the fresh, warm air and all this city has to offer.

My first stop is a cute boutique with all kinds of handmade goodies. Jewelry and hair accessories, designer handbags, scarves, and sunglasses line the walls and storefront. I barely walk in ten feet before a woman approaches me.

"Well, hello there." She greets me with a sweet, southern drawl. "How ya doing?"

"Fine, thank you." I smile back. "Your shop is gorgeous."

"Thank you." She beams with pride. "It's actually my mama's, but my sister, Cherise and I do most of the customer service duties now that she's inching toward retirement. Although she still does all the accountin' and orderin'," she tells me, but I don't know why.

I smile and nod as I run my fingers through one of the scarves on display. "The fabric is so soft."

"Oh, that's because my Aunt Jeannie—she lives across Cooper River o'er there—washes all the fabric in baby oil before sewing the patterns together. Then she steams them, but only using distilled water, and once they dry, she sprays them with organic fabric softener. It's a process, she says, but she enjoys it, so she keeps doin' it." She rambles fast, making it hard to process everything she's saying.

Blinking, I bite my lip and nod. "Wow, that's very cool." Oversharing must be common around here because you definitely won't get that in the Midwest.

Reading her nametag, I see her name is Cherry. Smiling, I walk around the shop as she continues telling me the backstory on every item I pick up. The pair of earrings her Aunt Mae designed, the sunglasses they found in Italy and can barely keep them in stock this time of year, the bracelet her Gram Gram redesigned from a bracelet her mama bought for her many years ago. With how much she talks, I could write an entire novel before I even get a chance to leave the store.

She asks my name and why I'm visiting. Once I tell her, she goes on and on about how she loved watching *My Girl* with her kids, who are named Christine and Caitlin, and then proceeds to tell me how she's read every single Nicholas Sparks novel to date after I tell her I'm a writer who's here on business.

By the time I make my way back to the front and checkout with a new scarf and pair of earrings—neither of which I really needed—I know all of Cherry's pets' names: Scruffy, Spinner, Spike, and Bella, as well as her thoughts on the annual Labor Day parade that's coming up. Granted, I was a little put off at first by a stranger telling me so many personal details, but by the time I leave, I've actually enjoyed the company—as weird as it was.

I continue walking down the street, the sun beaming down on me and decide to tie my hair up into a ponytail. Once I've managed to get the hair off my neck, I bend down to pick up my bags when I see the store sign across the street—Paris Pottery & Studio. Recognizing the name from the bottom of Casanova's mugs, I walk there next.

I'm in complete awe as I walk inside and look around. Everything looks so clean and artistic. Lining a dark navy-blue accent wall are wooden shelves stocked with clay mugs, bowls, and plates. On the other wall is a display of mugs, similar to the ones in Casanova's cupboard. I walk toward that side of the store before anyone can stop and tell me their life story.

A sign on display reads Original Paris Mug, and I pick one up and look at the bottom to see the same Paris logo.

"Those are South Carolina's most popular mugs," a female's voice comes from behind. I spin around and see a young woman smiling at me. Her name tag reads, Hilary. "Made locally right here in Charleston." She politely folds her hands in front and waits for me to speak.

"I borrowed one this morning actually," I tell her. "I was hoping to find one for myself."

"Sure, darling. Ethan has a large variety of mugs. I'm sure we can find one you'll like." She winks, reaching for one on the shelf. "No two are the same."

"Ethan?"

"The potter. It all started with the Original Paris mug. At first, they were only available online, and it was more of a hobby than a career. He would do live videos of him throwing clay, and people just went crazy over it. Not to mention, he's not bad to look at either." She winks, and I'm starting to notice a pattern. "His videos and mugs started blowing up the internet, and soon he was selling out every week."

"Wow, that's amazing," I say in complete admiration.

"Oh, that's just the beginnin', darling. An investor swooped in so he could make this a career and throw clay full-time. He continued making his mugs and customers wanted more. The demand was so high, he opened up this studio and hired interns to run it."

"So you're an intern?"

"Yep, from the art institution," she proudly responds.

I smile and nod, appreciating the history behind the mugs and studio.

She starts talking about the process of each one, and it's all fascinating and overwhelming at the same time. By the way, she talks about him, I imagine this Ethan guy to be early-thirties give or take, obviously good with his hands and gorgeous. If he's anything like Casanova, probably an arrogant asshole, too.

"So do you see anything you like?" she asks me, and after taking another look, I pick out two of my favorite.

"Make sure to hand-wash only," she reminds me as she hands me a cream-colored bag with the word *Paris* written in script on both sides. I love all the cute touches this shop has from the personal customer service, the easy shopping experience, and the modern look mixed with the southern decor gives it a rustic vibe.

"Will do," I promise. "I can't wait to bring these back to Chicago with me."

"Enjoy, sweetheart."

After thanking her again and grabbing my bag, I start to head out. Before I open the door, a plaque on the wall grabs my attention. A plaque with Casanova's face on it.

CHAPTER FOUR

ETHAN

BY THE TIME the sun sets, I'm absolutely fucking exhausted. Running a business—a successful one, at that—isn't easy. Regardless if it's my passion or not, I want nothing more than to go home, pour a glass of scotch, and sit in the garden. Usually, when I'm anxious or worked up, viewing the flowers and listening to the cicadas in the late afternoon help me relax.

As soon as I get home and walk in, I go straight to the kitchen, throw some ice cubes in a glass and pour a double of Johnny Walker Double Black. Wilma comes trotting down the stairs and rubs her body against my legs. Bending down, I pet her and place some treats on the floor before walking outside. She's too busy eating to even notice me leave.

Finally, I let out a deep breath. I sit on a bench close to the fountain I had installed last summer and listen to the water trickle down the rocks. Just as I put the glass to my lips, Vada comes waltzing by, and I swear she's purposely shaking her round ass. As soon as she turns around, I'm halfway through an eyeroll. I'm actually kind of getting used to her death glare.

"No hello or anything?" Her hands fall to her hips, and I have a feeling she's used to addressing people this way.

This woman has no filter and calls it like she sees it. After only twenty-four hours, she calls my bullshit like she's known me for years. Not many people point out my antics; most just look at me with sorrow in their eyes. I push those thoughts away as quickly as they came. Giving a smile that doesn't affect her in the least way, I realize I may have met my match.

"Just sitting out here enjoying the *peace and quiet*." The sarcasm isn't lost on her, and she takes a few steps forward, closer to me, just as I take a sip of scotch.

"I was always told southern men were gentlemen. Going forward, I'm going to argue with anyone who believes that and let them know how entirely wrong they are." She pauses for a moment, glaring at me. When I don't respond, she continues. "So now who's the one gawking?" she asks as she crosses her arms over her breasts.

I didn't realize I was staring until she spoke, but I brush it off. "Just returning the favor from yesterday."

She grinds her teeth. "Let me set the record straight. I wasn't gawking at you. I was confused that you were shirtless and wet. Most people don't answer a door like that. At least not where I'm from." She takes a step closer.

"Really? Most people don't shower where you're from? Hmm. Thought it was a common practice, you know, around the world."

I can tell she's getting annoyed as she narrows her eyes at me.

To add fuel to the fire and to see how worked up I can really get her, I remind her of the deadline she's been so worked up about since she arrived. "Don't you have a book to write?"

She scoffs. "Well Casanova, I'm actually a little uninspired after going to this crappy pottery shop downtown today. It was absolutely awful in there. You must've heard of it, considering you have a few of their pieces. Paris Pottery & Studio?"

I don't know if it's the scotch that's sending a burning sensation through me or her words, but somehow, I force out a smirk. One of those that make me look like a bigger asshole than I really am.

"Really? That's a shame," I say, completely unamused. She has to know I own the place and she's trying to get under my skin, but she can't play the player. Realizing she's not getting to me, she continues on complaining about nonexisting issues.

"The walls were terrible. The art was sad. The lady working there was rude as hell…"

I lift my eyebrows, allowing her to finish, and that's when I realize she's carrying a bag with an Eiffel Tower logo and the Paris inscription. A devious smile touches my lips, and I nod my head and listen to her make a complete ass out of herself. Once she's finished, I stand, set my glass down on the bench and yank the bag from her hand.

"What are you doing?" she squeals, finally realizing she's been holding it the entire time.

"Just seeing which awful piece you decided to waste your hard-earned porn money on."

Her mouth falls open, and I can tell she's offended. "I do *not* write porn."

Nodding my head, I peek inside and see two items wrapped in brown paper. Mugs. It's the only thing she could have bought. "That's not what Google says about you."

"You *did not* Google me."

My eyes meet hers for a brief moment as I carefully unwrap the brown paper from one of the items. She chose one of the most recent pieces I made one early morning a month or so ago. After looking out the tall windows that surround my office, I painted it the color of the sky just as the sun was rising. As she opens her mouth to say something else, I pretend to almost drop the mug, and she gasps trying to catch it.

"Just what I thought," I tell her as I carefully wrap and place it back into the bag and hand it to her.

With puckered lips, she looks up at the sky as if she's trying to pluck her words from the clouds. "Fine. You busted me. I know you're the owner of Paris Pottery & Studio. Are you happy?"

"I bet that was painful to say." I'm smiling—a genuine smile—as she stands there defeated that she didn't win this round.

"So now you're going to truthfully tell me your opinion about the shop, right?"

It's almost as if she's trying to force the words off her tongue. Her voice is so low that whatever she says is completely inaudible.

"I'm sorry. I didn't hear you," I say, cupping a palm around my ear.

She huffs. "I said, I loved it. Everything about the place was perfect. The selection, the art. I was actually shocked when I saw your picture there. I don't know why you just didn't say yesterday morning when I was admiring your work."

My face softens, and I relax. "Because it's not a quick conversation, and it's easier if we don't get personal."

Almost instantly, her demeanor changes as if my words offended her, but it's the truth. Getting personal with my tenant only causes problems, and she'll only be here for a week anyway. What's the point?

"Well okay then, Casanova. My sincerest apologies for being an ass about your shop. I should probably get back to writing my porn now. Have a good night, *Ethan*."

It's the first time she's said my name, and it almost sounds sweet coming from her lips. Vada turns and walks away, and before she closes the door to the cottage, I speak across the garden to her. "Goodnight, Vada."

The door to the cottage clicks closed, and I grab my glass from the bench and walk inside. Before heading upstairs for a shower, I pour the melted ice and scotch down the drain and bend over to pet Wilma who's begging for more treats. I tell her no and go upstairs to my workspace on the third story to make sure the kilns are amping down.

Unbuttoning my shirt, I stand at the large windows that surround the tower room and look out at the garden. It's so high up above everything, that it helps me forget the worries that follow me throughout the day. I almost feel as if I'm in the clouds. After checking a few of my pieces on the wooden boards and just as I'm about to turn around, my eyes wander to the cottage.

Expecting to see Vada working at the small desk, I'm shocked when she walks from the bathroom with nothing more than a towel wrapped around her tight body. She snaps the sheer curtains shut, and the towel drops to the floor in a crum-

27

pled pile. As she crosses the room, I swallow hard at the outline of her naked body. Not able to turn away, completely magnetized to her, I watch through the large skylight that's conveniently positioned above the bed. When she lies down, I know exactly where this is going.

Her dark, wet brown hair cascades on the pillow, and she looks like pure perfection with her soft skin against the white comforter. Vada closes her eyes, allowing her hands to roam to her nipples, and I memorize every curve she has. If I concentrate hard enough, I can almost hear the soft sound of her moans and breaths as she pinches and pulls at her nipples. I shouldn't be watching her, but then she moves one hand down to her clit, and there's no way I'm walking away now. Taking her time, she teases herself with slow circular movements while palming one of her perky breasts. I halfway wonder if she can sense my eyes glued to her because she's putting on one hell of a show for me.

Watching her and imagining the way she feels is making my dick so goddamn hard, I'm going to have to take care of this sooner than later. The woman is teasing herself with such fervor that I'm getting worked up, which isn't something that typically happens to me. Then again, I've never experienced a beautiful woman masturbating in my cottage with every light on, giving no fucks about anything but her pussy.

I'm halfway tempted to go over there and ask if she needs any help. Just as the thought crosses my mind, she opens her legs wider and slowly inserts a finger. No, she doesn't need any help. She actually has it all taken care of. *Fuck.*

Vada is careful with herself, moving her fingers along her wet slit before inserting them back inside, over and over again.

The rhythmic motions as she sinks deeper and deeper is driving me fucking insane. She's an expert at pleasing herself, and now I'm curious about the sex scenes in her books.

When her back arches and she picks up the pace, I know she's teetering on the edge. I wait with bated breath for her release as she continues to simultaneously finger fuck herself and rub her clit. Without slowing down, she gives her pussy exactly what it deserves, working herself to completion. She bites down on her bottom lip as the orgasm violently rushes through her, causing her body to buckle on the bed. Her mouth falls open, and I know she's moaning loudly, allowing the moment to take full control of her. Continuing to ride the euphoric wave until the very last moment, her body eventually relaxes, and it's the sexiest thing I've ever witnessed. I can only imagine how wet she is and the urge to want to taste her over-comes and shocks the shit out of me.

Her breasts rise and fall, and a small smile hits her lips as she exhales, completely satisfied with what she accomplished. With flushed cheeks and nipples as hard as pebbles, she lies there without a care in the world. Vada's beautiful and mesmer-izing, and I can't seem to pull away from her. Though she doesn't have a filter on that mouth of hers, I find myself fanta-sizing about being inside her, giving her everything she can't possibly give herself sexually. My heart pounds so hard in my chest as her naked body stretches across the bed, and I can't deny this feeling inside me. It's raw. It's pure lust and hunger. Once her breathing steadies, she slides off the bed, puts on a robe then sits at the desk. Opening her laptop, she begins typing away with a shit-eating grin on her face. I can only imagine the words she's writing at this very moment. *Dirty girl.*

Somehow, I force myself away from the windows and walk downstairs to my bedroom, but the images of her and the look on her face as she came won't stop replaying in my head. My dick throbs so hard in my jeans that it's almost painful. Heading to the bathroom, I begin disrobing, dropping my clothes along the way. Once I turn on the water and step in, I close my eyes and grab my dick that's as hard as steel. As the water runs down my body, I grab myself in long strokes. Trying to steady myself, I place a hand on the wall, picking up the pace, feeling the orgasm ready to rip through me. Everything about her fills my mind. Moments later, my body is convulsing with the quickest orgasm I've had in years, and it's all because of that smart-mouthed writer and her perfect pussy. If only she could write about that.

CHAPTER FIVE

VADA

I WAKE UP REFRESHED and happy with my word count for the night. It wasn't my personal best, but the few thousand words I was able to type bring me closer to my goal.

The morning starts off hectic with a call from my agent. Hannah is one of those ladies who is all business, and for most of the call, she hounds me for my manuscript, but it's still in draft mode, so I can't send her what she wants just yet. She really has my best interest in mind, but considering I'm already behind, it all adds to my stress level. I've never been late sending a book to my agent, and I don't plan on starting now. By the time I get off the phone, I'm a bit deflated and realize how badly I need coffee. The day just started, and I can tell it's going to be a long one.

After I brush my teeth, I head over to Ethan's house to grab a cup of coffee. Before opening the door, I look through the window and see he's standing at the stove scrambling eggs and frying bacon, and it smells so divine.

Unfortunately for me, he's wearing nothing but a pair of jogging pants that are hanging off his hips. Muscles cascade down his back, and I can't help but admire his biceps. Realizing I'm staring just a little too long, I make my presence known.

"I didn't realize you were so domestic," I say, entering like I own the place. He watches me as I walk to the cupboard, grabbing one of his beautiful mugs from the cabinet and pouring myself a hot cup of coffee. As soon as the caffeine hits my lips, I can't help but let out a moan. It's hot and strong, just the way I like the heroes in my books.

His brows shoot up as he continues studying me. "Do you always moan so loud in the morning or do you reserve that for when the sun goes down?"

I roll my eyes as I take a seat at the bar. I don't know what the hell he's referring to, but I'm not taking any of his crap this morning. Soon he's plating the food, sets it in front of me, then proceeds to cook himself more.

"You didn't have to. I was going to go out and grab some breakfast," I tell him, forcing myself not to devour it with my hands like a savage because it smells so good.

He looks over his shoulder and speaks. "Down here, we just say thank you. Now eat it. Swear it's not poisoned."

When he turns back around to flip the bacon, I can't help but smile. You don't have to tell me twice. "Fine." I swallow hard, forcing my eyes to look away from him. "Thank you."

The eggs practically melt in my mouth, and the bacon is the way I like it, not burnt but crisp. By the time I'm halfway done eating, he finishes cooking and sets his food down across from me at the table. As he walks over to pour himself a cup of coffee, his bare chest and the muscles on his stomach taunt me. Seriously, this man should be on the cover of a book. Hell, he should be *in* a book.

"So'd you have a late night last night?" Ethan asks as he takes a bite of his eggs. The tone of his voice makes me narrow my eyes at him. After being a complete ass yesterday, I'm trying to not let out every thought that's on my mind.

"Actually, I did. Finished a chapter I've been working on for a few days. I think the fresh air and country living atmosphere is really helping me," I say honestly, trying to keep it cordial.

"Hm." Ethan snaps a piece of bacon in half and takes a bite. "Want to know what I think is helping you?"

I roll my eyes again, knowing some smart-ass comment is about to come from his mouth. "Please, Casanova. Enlighten me," I say, taking a big gulp of coffee.

"Maybe it was that intense orgasm you gave yourself that helped you write all night."

I almost spit my coffee out all over him and hurry to swallow it down. My eyes nearly bug out of my head, and I'm tempted to slap that smirk right off his face. I'm shocked and somewhat embarrassed.

"What?" I shake my head at him, trying to deny it. "What are you talking about?" I act dumb, hoping he's just messing with me and trying to get me all riled up like usual. I try to pretend last night never happened. But what the fuck? Does he have cameras in there or something? Sometimes when the words aren't flowing, having a release helps loosen me up. When I get tense or stressed, I tend to get blocked. So, last night it *really* helped.

"Come on, Vada. You don't have to get all uptight." He continues eating, his eyes meeting mine. "Honestly, I thought it was pure fucking perfection. So damn hot."

My body is on fire because no one has ever watched me touch myself. Often when it comes to sex, although I write about it all the time, I'm a private person. Heat rushes to my face. Ethan saw me completely exposed and vulnerable.

I stand, getting ready to walk away when he comes around the bar and grabs my hand. With strong arms, he spins me around until my body is close to his bare chest. He smells like vanilla and holds me in place, not allowing me to move.

"You're an asshole for watching. Do you have a spy cam in there or something? Are you some sort of perv who likes to watch his renters?"

Ethan tightens his grip on me, and his arms fall to his sides. "Did you feel the sun beat down on your body this morning?"

That's when the skylight above the bed dawns on me. "So you played Spider Man and was climbing on the roof? That's so creepy."

Shaking his head, he smiles. "My work area is in the tower on the third floor. There's a direct view into the cottage. I couldn't take my eyes away from you. The look on your face as you came; so fucking hot. But I couldn't help noticing that you could've used some help. There's nothing like the real deal, sweetheart."

"And what, you're the real deal?" I bark out a laugh. "You're a dickhead for watching." I glare at him and wait.

"Okay, I'm sorry," he finally says, sincerely. I can tell he means it, but it still doesn't take away what he saw. I never would've imagined I could be seen from a distance like that.

Otherwise, there's no way I would've put on a show. Especially for *him*.

"That was private and not for you." I poke my finger hard into his chest to really get my point across. "Southern gentleman, my ass. A gentleman would've walked away."

He laughs out loud. "No way. No man would've turned a blind eye to that unless the ladies aren't his thing. That's the only way. So yes, even a gentleman would've watched. In fact, if I weren't a gentleman, I would've stalked over and joined in."

I gasp at his words, so bold and honest. Though I'm pissed that the moment wasn't as private as I thought, knowing he watched and enjoyed it is doing unusual things to my body. Tingles rush through me, and I feel exhilarated from it all, but even so, I want nothing more than to escape from his presence. He's way too close for comfort, and the way he's looking at me with soft eyes is...*different*.

"I said, I'm sorry. Accept it or not," he tells me before walking back to his breakfast.

I suck in a deep breath and go back to my plate of food and finish eating without saying a word while Ethan's eyes are glued to me. When I look up at him, he's smiling, chewing with his mouth open.

"Have some manners, at least. Not only are you an ass, but you're disgusting, too." As always, my words don't faze him. He stands and places his plate in the sink then walks around and grabs mine. His arm brushes against my skin and goose bumps trail up and down my body. Tucking my arms in my lap, I don't dare give him any fuel to add to his country bumpkin bonfire because he's enjoying this way too much.

I'm intrigued, but I don't say a word. Sometimes the silent treatment is more powerful than saying what's on my mind.

Turning around, he gives me a smirk as he leans against the counter. "So one more question for you. What time should I be in the tower tonight? Same as last night?"

"You're seriously one of the biggest douchebags I've ever met."

"Oh, come on. That can't be true. I'm sure you've met bigger ones." He grins, knowing he's getting under my skin.

"Sometimes I get anxious or restless, and I need a release to help me relax and concentrate so I can get back to work. It clears my mind, so I don't overthink while writing. There's nothing wrong with it. Nothing at all. So quit bringing it up. It happened, and it's over. Get over it. Next time, I'll make sure to take a nice long bath instead. There's no spy windows in there." I'm so annoyed, I walk across the kitchen to pour coffee in my cup that I plan on taking to-go.

"Shit, you must get yourself off several times during the day then, because uptight seems to be your middle name." Ethan chuckles.

I roll my eyes so hard they might actually fall right out of my head.

"Shut up, Ethan." There's too many words to write, and I'm wasting too much time with him. Just as I head to the door, he speaks up again.

"Vada." He walks to me, allowing himself into my personal space. I take a step backward, which only causes him to take another step forward. "Any time you need to be unwound, just let me know." His voice is low, rough, and so damn sexy that my mouth falls open.

I look into his eyes and can tell he's actually fucking serious. My face contorts, and I look at him like he's lost his damn mind. "Seriously? Is this the part where I'm supposed to fall on my knees for you?"

"You're the author here. Tell me how you'd write the story," he quips.

I pretend to throw up in my mouth.

"Goddamn, you're always so feisty. I kinda like that, you know."

I huff. "I don't know you, and you sure as hell don't know me. I'm not some whore at your service. That's not who I am. But then again, I'm paying you, so that'd make you my whore if we were to get technical here."

Slowly, Ethan brushes his fingers across my cheek and tucks my messy morning hair behind my ear. Those stupid tingles creep across my body, and it takes everything I have not to lean into his touch.

Leaning over, he whispers in my ear. "Sex doesn't have to be like one of those romantic scenes in your books. Sometimes it can be purely physical with no strings attached." His breath runs along my skin, and his mouth barely grazes the shell of my ear causing me to shiver. As he pulls away, I feel as if I'm unable to move, glued to the floor, holding my mug as tight as I can so I don't drop it. Swallowing hard, I try to catch the breath he somehow stole.

Snapping out of it and finally finding my words, I think of the perfect response. "So do you offer your dick to all the women who rent your cottage? If so, you should really update your Airbnb listing. *Country cottage comes with amenities, such as beautiful views, flower gardens, and gigolo services.* Probably could get double your rate."

Ethan crosses his strong arms over his chest and smirks. This time, the way he's looking at me with those honey-colored eyes practically make my panties melt off my body. Seriously, I'm surprised there's not a line of women waiting at his door. But being the bad boy I know he is, he's probably screwed and scared them all away.

"Actually, sweetheart," he starts, sucking in a breath. "You'd be the first." Ethan chews on his plump bottom lip before taking a sip of coffee.

Dead. I'm dead, but I have to pull it together before I do something stupid and spontaneous. *Like accept his ridiculous offer.*

"Right. I *really* believe that. It's been real fun, but I gotta go, Casanova. Try not to offer your dick to too many women today while you're out and about. It might fall off or something."

Before I close the door, I hear him loudly chuckling, and it drives me absolutely insane. He's enjoying this way too much, and it's bothering the shit out of me because nothing I say remotely affects him. It takes everything I have to not turn around and give him a piece of my mind, but he'd probably like it. Considering I've dealt with his type before, and I don't want to end up having rough, crazy sex on the kitchen floor with him, walking away is the best decision.

Once I'm in the cottage, I sip my coffee while sitting back at the desk and turn on my laptop. I reread the previous chapter, trying to get back into my headspace, but I'm drawing nothing. At this point, I've gone completely off my outline, and no words are coming to me. There's nothing but a cursor on a blank page. This chapter and two others have to be written today, which is thousands of words. I stare up at the ceiling, trying to concentrate then crack my fingers and place them back on the keyboard.

Blink. Blink. Blink.

That stupid cursor is mocking me.

A few hours pass and I write a lousy paragraph that I end up deleting. Hannah's words are repeating in my mind, and I remind myself that she's rooting for me and my career. Basically, I just need to get my shit together. My last book didn't sell as well as I had hoped, or my publisher expected, so if I don't knock it out of the park with this new project, my writing career may be doomed. There's no way I'm going back to the corporate world. Writing is my calling, my passion, and I have to make this work. Closing my eyes tight, I hope the words will just flow through my fingers like magic.

Blink. Blink. Blink. I'm two seconds away from banging my head against the desk, and after six long hours of getting nothing done, I'm becoming more desperate. This day cannot be wasted. I need words at this point like I need air.

All my anxiety and stress about this deadline is mixing with Casanova's words. He basically presented me his dick on a gold platter. *Probably all hard and thick with bulging veins and a velvet-soft shaft.* Fuck. Maybe he was kidding or baiting me, but when I looked into his eyes, I knew deep down he was serious.

There was no joking.

No animosity.

That man meant what he said with every fiber of his being. But the truth is, girls like me don't go for bad boys like him. Our types clash. Always.

CHAPTER SIX

ETHAN

THOUGH VADA ACTED like my proposal disgusted her, I can read her like a newspaper. She's secretly thinking about my offer while trying to talk herself out of it.

I can't really blame her though. I've never done anything like this before, especially in my community where everyone knows of me, my family, and my studio. After Alana, everyone treated me like a broken soul. They weren't wrong. I was broken. Truthfully, I still feel broken from everything that was taken away from me.

Instead of dwelling on what happened, I buried myself into my work. Worked harder, faster, and longer. It was the only thing that kept me from falling apart most days, and even when I started to have success in my art, the fear of failing again never drifted.

One-night stands were strictly that—one night. I haven't committed to anyone since Alana, and I doubt I'll ever be able to.

The only priorities I have in life now are my work and family. I know my momma would like it if I settled down, but after getting the same response from me for the past few years, she's learned to stop asking.

After Vada stalks out and I clean up the kitchen, I head upstairs to the tower and start my morning work routine. I don't bother putting a shirt on because the sun is already beating down on me. With how the windows surround the tower, there's no way to escape the heat. I could wait till after the sun sets to work, but I'm feeling oddly inspired today.

I gather up my materials, tools, and block of clay. Once I've prepared the clay and wedged and smacked all the air bubbles out, I sit down at the potter's wheel and begin wetting my sponge. Pressing my foot down on the accelerator, I squeeze the sponge above the bat to wet the surface. I continue this until it's smooth and free of clay from the previous use.

Once that's all set, I throw my prepared block of clay as close to the middle of the bat as I can. This process used to take me a good half hour to get it centered correctly, but after doing it for years, it now only takes a few minutes. Wetting my hands, I begin centering by raising and lowering the clay as the wheel spins. Once it's ready to go, I start my process for making a Paris mug. I push my thumb down into the middle to form the opening, and once I have it just the way I like it, I use my tools to etch and design the outside.

Once it's ready to go, I use my cutting wire and slide it under the mug. I pick up the bat and set the entire thing on one of my shelves. Grabbing another bat, I repeat the entire process until I have twenty mugs complete. Next, I'll add the handles.

Standing up and stretching, I crack my neck and twist my waist from side to side. Working on the wheel and slouching over tends to make my lower back muscles stiff and achy, which is why I usually take a long, hot shower at night.

I head downstairs and make another pot of coffee. While waiting for it to brew, I whip together a quick sandwich and eat before I head back upstairs. Staring out the windows, I overlook the property while taking sips of my coffee. I notice movement in the cottage and see Vada sitting at the desk, but her fingers aren't flying across the keyboard like I expect. Instead, they're massaging her temples in slow circular movements. She's obviously frustrated. A moment later, she slams her laptop shut and leans back in the chair.

I imagine lots of cursing and groaning, and I anxiously wait to see if she'll come to her senses about my offer. Wondering if she'll take matters into her own hands again, I wait and watch as I finish off my coffee. She ends up grabbing a few things from her suitcase before locking herself in the bathroom.

Assuming she's going to be in there a while, enjoying the handheld shower head sprayer, I get back to work for a few hours. Once I've put handles on the mugs and inscribe my Paris logo onto the bottoms, I break to freshen up and grab some water. My chest and jeans are covered in wet clay, as usual, but before I head upstairs to shower, I hear a shriek from the back garden.

"Go away! Stop chasing me!" Vada screams, and as soon as I see who she's screaming at, I crack up and laugh my ass off.

"He's harmless," I tell her as soon as I open the back door and step out. "That's how Henry shows affection." I smirk, knowing she's not seeing the humor in any of this.

"A rooster who wanders around your yard pecking at my ankles is not affection!" She scowls. "I nearly fell on my face running from him."

"Stop running, and he'll stop chasing," I simply explain.

"Easy for you to say." She steps closer to the house to avoid Henry. "Do you have any idea how terrifying it is to have a rooster-creature terrorize you?"

Scratching my fingernails along my jawline, I suck in my lower lip to hold back what I really want to say. "And you call yourself a writer."

"Shut up. You know what I mean. Control your huge..." She lingers, and I don't miss the opportunity to fill in the word for her.

"Cock?" My eyebrows rise.

She groans and rolls her eyes at me. "Seriously. This is why I don't socialize with people."

"Yeah, I'm sure that's why you're an introvert."

"Hey, you don't know anything about me, okay?" she reminds me, and it's the truth, but I'm not going to let her off that easy.

"I might not know a lot about you, but I know some."

"Like what?" She crosses her arms, challenging me. "What could you possibly know about me in just three days?"

Leaning my body against the doorframe, I smirk and think back to last night and how her body sang after she got herself off. I haven't been able to get it out of my mind actually.

"I know you're as uptight as you look. City girl, isolated, with a lack of social skills. You have your guard up even when it's not merited. You don't let people in because of something that happened in your past, more than likely.

You'd rather form relationships in your books than in real life."

"I'm not uptight." She tries defending herself, but I continue anyway.

"You're so uptight you have to touch yourself to relax. I know it took you approximately three minutes to get off. You know just where to touch and how you like it because it's the only relief you allow yourself to have. You arch your back just when you feel it coming, and I know you'd enjoy it more if you'd actually get fucked hard like you need."

Her jaw drops, her eyes narrowing as she stares intently at me. I can tell she's trying to find the words to respond, but she closes her mouth and swallows.

"Come in." I smile. "I'll make dinner."

I don't wait for her to reply and turn around to go back inside the house. She follows behind, silently, and when she closes the door, I glance back at her and can see her mind racing a million miles a minute.

Digging around the fridge, I pull out two chicken breasts. She watches me as I wash and cut them into cubes. We stay silent as I move around the kitchen and prepare dinner. Adding a box of rice to the cooked chicken, I cover the pan and let it simmer.

"Do you cook for all your tenants?" she blurts out as I grab two plates from the cupboard.

"No," I say, grabbing the utensils next. "I haven't cooked for someone in a long time."

"Why's that?" she urges.

"You really want to know?" I ask, directing my eyes at her

in warning. She won't like what she hears, but I won't lie about it either.

"Yes."

Clearing my throat, I set the plates and forks on the table where she's sitting.

"Most tenants don't stay around the cottage all day. They're usually here to explore and go to the beach. They eat out, and I only see them at check-in and check-out."

"Okay?" she says as a question. "What about family or friends?"

"Not really. My mama and aunt are usually the ones to bring me food. Not a lot of time to socialize with friends."

"Which means you have none." She grins.

"I do. Most of them come over after dinnertime."

"Ohh…you mean, chicks. You could've just said that." She tries to keep a straight face, but I can tell it's close to breaking.

"I didn't think I needed to."

"So if you don't cook for tenants or booty calls, why do you cook for me?"

"Because even though you're an uptight city girl, I enjoy your company."

"That almost sounded like a compliment." She smiles.

I shrug with a smirk and get up to check on the chicken and rice. I turn the burner off and bring the pan to the table.

"Thank you," she says after I plate her food and set it down in front of her.

"You'd probably starve without me," I tease her.

She chuckles, not denying it. "Probably true. The writer's diet is no joke. I'm either eating everything in sight, or I forget to eat entirely."

"Sounds like my entire college career," I admit, remembering all the times I'd be scraping for change.

Halfway through dinner, I bring up my offer again. Mostly to taunt her, but also because I'm hoping she's changed her mind. I can't get the image of her touching herself out of my head, and I'd be lying if I said I wasn't curious about the way she tastes when she comes.

"Even if I was desperate enough to sleep with you, which I'm *not*, I don't have sex with guys I just met."

"Even good-looking ones?"

She starts choking on a mouthful of food, and that's all the answer I need.

"That's what I thought." I stab my last piece of chicken and shove it into my mouth as I watch her expression tighten.

"I was choking because you think so highly of yourself, not because I was agreeing," she clarifies, and though she's trying to sound serious, I see the corner of her lips tilt up.

Standing up, I take our plates to the sink and rinse them off. I feel her walk toward me and take the opportunity to spin around and face her.

"So how do you know if you've never done it before?" I ask, taking a step forward when she takes a step back.

"Know what?"

"How do you know you wouldn't enjoy yourself?"

"Because I know myself. I need to know someone to be intimate with them on a physical level," she explains, although I'm not convinced.

"You sure about that?" I ask, closing the gap between us until our bodies press against each other. Before she can respond, I cover her mouth with mine, and though she's taken off guard, only seconds pass before her body relaxes.

Slipping my tongue between her plump lips, she moans as I devour her. Cupping her cheek, I hold her in place as I taste her sweetness. Our bodies lean against each other, and a smirk forms on my lips when I feel her fingers digging into my hips, craving more.

I sink my tongue deeper, hearing another hungry moan release from her throat. I knew she'd taste good, but fuck, her moans and sweetness are better than I imagined. My cock throbs against the inside of my jeans, begging to be released.

Pulling back, I feel her heavy breathing against my chest. She looks up at me with swollen lips as her chest moves rapidly.

"If you change your mind, you know where to find me." I wink, releasing her body and walking out of the kitchen.

CHAPTER SEVEN

VADA

I'M PRETTY sure I need CPR or some kind of life-saving equipment.

I can't seem to catch my breath, even though I'm breathing just fine, but the way he just kissed me and then walked away has my mind reeling and my body confused as hell.

His lips were so warm and inviting, I couldn't stop. I didn't *want* to pull away, and that's even more confusing to me than I like admitting. However, I can't deny the way his kiss affected me. The way his body pressed against mine or how *my* body responded like I was some desperate sex-deprived woman.

I'm not, by the way. *Stupid, traitorous body.*

I'm still trying to catch my breath when I leave and walk out the back door. Quickly glancing around to make sure Henry isn't following me again, I walk the garden path and head inside the cottage.

I don't have time to think about Ethan and that kiss, I remind myself.

48

I don't have time to analyze the way that kiss made me feel, I also remind myself.

But fuck. It was a *really* good kiss.

But why did he kiss me? And why did I kiss him back?

Ugh! How dare he kiss me like that!

My mind is all over the place, and I can't keep up with my own thoughts. His proposal repeats in my head. I'm trying to forget his offer while talking myself into considering it. Contradiction plagues me. Would it really be so bad to have one night of fun while I'm here?

What am I even saying?

I palm my forehead, trying to smack the oxygen back into my brain.

This man is making me second-guess everything I believe, and it's driving me absolutely crazy! I write about heroines who have one-night stands or who fuck a guy after just meeting them, but that isn't real life. At least not for me. I've seen firsthand what jumping into a relationship based on sex can do to a couple, and it isn't pretty.

Deciding to march back over there, I don't bother knocking before letting myself in. I stomp my way upstairs even though I have no idea where he went, but I'm not thinking straight anymore. My heart is racing, and I'm determined to give him a piece of my mind. *Who does he think he is kissing me like that?*

There are two doors on each side of the hallway, and one is cracked halfway open, so I decide to try that one first.

"Ethan!" I shout. My bare feet thump against the hardwood floor as I try to find him. I peek around the barely open door, which ends up being the bathroom. "Ethan, where are you?" I raise my voice louder, not sure if I should try the other doors or not.

I step farther down the hallway and hear bass thumping along the ceiling. He must be in the tower.

Rounding the corner, I spot the stairs that lead up to the third floor. The music becomes louder as I quietly take the steps. When I reach the top, I see his bare muscular back hunched over slightly as his hands work a chunk of clay on his pottery wheel. It's loud and vibrates the floors, which is probably why his music is as loud as it is.

Wooden boards surround the room with clay mugs and bowls. Large white buckets are scattered around the room with *glaze* written on them, and it looks like a great working space. So peaceful and probably has a gorgeous view in the early mornings.

I watch him for a while, admiring the way his muscles contract in his biceps as he shifts in his seat between wetting the sponge and molding the clay between his fingers. I've never seen anyone make pottery before, but he makes it seem effortless. Actually, really fucking sexy. Studying him, I don't realize how long it's been, and when he shifts his body and glances at me, his face contorts. I expect him to scold me for watching when he didn't know, but instead, he scoots back on the seat and tilts his head.

"Come sit," he orders.

At first, I think I hear him wrong, the music must've jumbled his words, but when he jerks his head again, I know I didn't.

Licking my lips, I take a step and walk toward him. He sits

back just enough to allow me to sit in front of him, basically *in* his lap, but I don't complain.

His arms wrap around mine, and he guides my hands to the clay in the middle of his wheel. Pressing his foot on the pedal, the wheel begins to spin again. His hands cover mine as we shape the clay, and he uses his finger to guide my thumb into the middle where a hole starts to form.

"I hope I don't mess up your piece," I turn my head slightly and tell him loud enough, so he can hear me.

His body maneuvers closer to mine, his chest against my back leaving no space between us. My body shivers at the close contact and how he's holding me in place with his thighs and shoulders.

"You probably will," he whispers, and even though his tone is serious, I feel his lips spread into a smirk against the shell of my ear.

I chuckle, leaning my body against his for support, not wanting to admit how good it feels to have him so close to me. I came up here to yell at him, and now his bare chest has captured my body, and unwillingly—my heart. He slowly removes his hands and slides them up my arms before reaching for his sponge. After wetting it, he squeezes it over my hands and clay.

Feeling his lips press softly against my neck, my eyes flutter as I lose focus. The scruff from his beard tickles my skin, and I feel myself unraveling. His hands slowly slide up my arms, leaving streaks of dirty clay water along them. My throat goes dry as his hand firmly wraps around my neck and tilts my face toward his. Warm lips capture my mouth, and I easily fall into his embrace. His tongue glides with mine, and soon the wheel is no longer spinning as my hands wrap around his wrists for support in a silent plea to not stop anytime soon.

His thumb rubs along my jawline as our kiss deepens, and as much as I don't want to, I know I should stop. Except I can't. His kiss is so fucking good, so controlled, yet desperate and eager. The way he holds me to him, the strength of his arms and body have me so entranced, I can't do anything except fall into his embrace.

"I've finally figured out what shuts you up," he teases against my mouth, a smirk playing on his lips. "Turns out it was keeping your tongue busy."

"If that's your version of sexy talk, I'm not impressed," I mock, barely audible.

"Your nipples say otherwise." He lowers his hand and plucks my taut nipple along the fabric of my shirt. "Hard and aroused. And I know it's not because of the weather."

"I really want to prove you wrong, but I know the farther your hand goes, the more right you'll be." The words bravely come out before I can stop them.

Leaning in, he bites down on my lower lip, causing a surge of electricity to spark through me. The last guy I briefly dated never made me feel this way, and Ethan has barely touched me.

A moan escapes my throat, and I feel him smile against my lips. *Fuck*. Now he definitely knows he's affecting me—not that I could really deny it anymore.

Keeping my face over my shoulder, he continues exploring my mouth as his hands pin my back to his chest. Even though the position is awkward, I don't make an effort to move. I love the way he's possessively holding me, my ass pressed between his thighs and rubbing against his cock.

Several moments pass of his lips and teeth teasing me before he presses his forehead to mine as we both try and catch our breaths. His hands roam my arms, neck, and face, and I now look like a living piece of art.

"We should clean up," he suggests, though not making an effort to move.

"That's probably a good idea," I agree, half-winded.

He backs off the stool and stretches his hand out for me to grab it. I place it in his, and he leads me downstairs. Following behind, I notice when he walks past the bathroom.

"I thought we were going to clean up," I say stupidly, assuming he was going to take us to the shower. I've let my guard down but am second-guessing myself now.

"We are," is all he says, leading me down the next set of stairs until we're on the main floor.

I can't deny how his mysterious tone sends butterflies straight to my stomach. I hardly know anything about this man, yet that doesn't stop me from following him.

We stay silent as we walk hand in hand to the front door and step out onto the wraparound porch. He continues leading me down the steps and onto the sidewalk, still giving me no indication of what he's up to.

Only walking a couple blocks, I finally see where he's taking me.

"What are we doing?" I ask, staring out at the creek.

He releases my hand and faces me. He smirks as he starts unbuttoning his jeans. "Cleaning up." He nods his head at me and continues, "Strip."

"Excuse me, what?" I gasp, taking a step back and thinking he must be crazy. "Out here?" Granted we're in an isolated area, surrounded by trees and water, but that doesn't mean other people couldn't be out here as well.

"C'mon, city girl. Afraid to get dirty in the country?" He arches a brow, challenging me.

I know he's mocking me, considering we're already both dirty, but by the way he's looking at me, I know he means it in an entirely different way.

I'm gettin' dirty in the south with Ethan Rochester.

"I see more of that southern charm is coming out," I tease, deciding to call his bluff and pull off my shirt. There's no way he's going to strip down to nothing.

"Down here we call it skinny dipping." He winks, kicking off his shoes before sliding his jeans down to his ankles and taking them off too.

"No," I say firmly, taking a step back. "I'm not going in there naked. With you."

"Why not? Afraid you'll actually have fun?"

I suck in a deep breath, my eyes gazing down his body—his beautiful, hard body. He's everything I write about in my books. Undeniably hot. Cocky attitude. Abs of steel that could cut my teeth. Hair shaggy on one side that makes me want to run my fingers through it as I straddle him. Mesmerizing eyes and lips that take over my senses every time I close my eyes. He's your typical bad boy hero, down to the ear piercings and rough scruff along his jawline that has me fantasizing how he'd feel between my legs.

Shit.

I've spent the last few years pushing men like him away, knowing they were bad news, yet here I'm standing in front of Mr. Bad News himself and not running away.

"Fine," I bite out. Two can play this game.

I unbutton my shorts and slide them down to my ankles before kicking them into the pile in front of us. Standing in only my bra and panties, I feel him studying me. His eyes slowly trace over my chest and move down my stomach and legs. When his eyes slide back up to mine, there's a knowing smirk taking place of his serious one.

His fingers wrap around the waistband of his boxer shorts, and I inhale deeply as he slowly peels them off. I tell myself to look away, but I can't. His eyes pin me to him, daring me to look away. Bending down, he pulls the shorts all the way to his ankles before standing back up and showing me the *whole* package.

Sweet fucking hell.

His ear isn't the only thing that's pierced.

Blinking, I swallow and try to act as if I am keeping it together. His cock should be packaged with a red ribbon tied around it because the way it hangs between his legs is like a gift to all women. Not to mention, I'm shamelessly curious how a piercing would feel inside me.

I want to make some kind of joke about it being cold outside and insinuate I'm not impressed by his size, but I'm fairly certain my voice would crack and completely blow my cover. My throat is so dry, I'm not sure I could form coherent words even if I tried.

His cock is thick. Thicker than I've ever seen and without staring at it too long, I shift my eyes away. I hear him chuckle as if my reaction to his naked body is funny.

"What?" I snap my eyes back to his, although I can see his cock in my peripheral vision. It's there all thick and big, and it might as well have a huge neon sign on it that says *Look at me! I'm your wet fantasy!*

"You act like you've never seen a naked man before."

I glare at him, making sure to keep my eyes above his waist.

"Wait. You have, right?" he asks, stepping closer.

"I'm twenty-seven years old. I've seen a naked man before," I snap.

"Then why are you acting like I have a poisonous snake between my legs?"

"Snake," I repeat with a laugh. "Sounds appropriate," I mutter to myself, though I'm sure he heard me.

"You want to feel it?" he asks, palming his fingers around it as he takes another step closer.

"What?" I gasp, blinking my eyes back to his and making sure I heard him correctly.

"The creek," he clarifies, but I know his purpose was to shock me. "It's like bath water."

"Oh." I swallow again, wishing my throat would stop feeling so damn dry. This guy has turned me into an idiot.

"Are you going to go in like that?" He jerks his head down to my bra and panties.

Looking at him, I try and find the courage to follow suit. I've already had to give myself permission to have fun this week, but I'm not sure this is a good idea. In fact, I *know* it's not a good idea. A guy like him could ruin me, and that's something I've promised myself since I was a teenager that I'd never let happen since watching my father verbally and emotionally abuse my mother for years.

You're a worthless piece of shit, and maybe if you ever took that stick out of your ass, you'd actually be a joy to be around. My father's words repeat in my head for the hundredth time since he's said them to my mother years ago. I hate how I allow his words to get to me even after all this time. I force them away when they surface, but I don't know why they've surfaced now.

I push his ugly words away and wrap my arms behind my back, so I can unhook my bra. Ethan watches me, and when my bra slides down my arms, he arches a brow.

"What?"

He rubs along his scruffy jawline, a noticeable smile charming his lips. "Keep going," he tells me, having no shame as he stares intently at my breasts.

I hook my fingers in my panties then slide them down my legs before adding them to our clothes pile. Thank God I waxed before this trip, which was mostly because I had a gift certificate to use at the salon before it expired. A birthday present from Nora who gets on me for my lack of self-care since I've starting writing full-time.

"No carpet, huh? Interesting."

I roll my eyes, shaking my head and pinching my lips together, so he doesn't see me smiling. He's totally eye-fucking my body, and it feels good knowing someone appreciates it.

"Only during the winter months when we Midwesterners need to stay warm," I tease as he grabs my hand and walks us down to the water.

"Remind me to never visit during cold season."

"Oh my God," I say, bursting into laughter as the water hits my ankles. "Wow…it is warm."

"I told you." He turns and winks, pulling us deeper into the water until it's up to my breasts.

"I guess you did." I roll my eyes. "At least the view was worth it."

"I'd have to agree with you on that one actually." He pulls me close until our chests are pressed together.

"I meant the sunset," I correct him with fake annoyance in my tone. "You're so egotistical." I shake my head.

"So did I," he corrects with a knowing grin. He's such a fucking liar. "Now who's egotistical?"

"I'd believe you if you weren't staring so hard at my chest."

"Well, you have nice tits. They're distracting."

"My tits are distracting?" I ask with laughter. "You want to touch them?"

His eyebrows shoot up, probably wondering if it's a trick or not. When I don't waver, he licks his lips and clears his throat.

"What happened to you not being desperate enough to sleep with a man like me?"

Pinching my lips together, I try to think of the perfect comeback, but nothing clever comes to mind. Probably because every time I glance at him, his gorgeous pierced cock invades my brain.

So my tits are distracting to him, and his cock has me thinking all kinds of bad and inappropriate thoughts.

The irony isn't lost on me.

"I decided to throw out all my standards," I finally answer. It's not a complete lie, but it's not the whole truth either. I'd be a fool to not want to sleep with a man like him. He can probably do things to me I've only ever written about or dreamed about, and even then, I don't always write those scenes based on experience. Sometimes it's based on fantasy, pure imagination, or porn.

"Are you saying I don't meet your standards?" he asks, offended.

"Quite the opposite, actually. I didn't mean physical standards, I meant emotionally. I came back over to yell at you for kissing me and then when you kissed me again, I don't know... I didn't want to use the energy to fight it any longer."

Keeping his eyes focused on mine, he brushes his finger along my jawline and to my cheek before moving strands of hair behind my ear. My long hair sticks to my shoulders and back, but that doesn't stop his urge to touch me. Keeping his hand cupped along my jaw, he pulls me forward until our lips connect. My hands wrap around his waist and hold onto him as if I'll drown without his support.

It'd be worth it, though.

CHAPTER EIGHT

ETHAN

KISSING VADA admittedly does something to me, but I can't quite put my finger on it. During these past few days of getting to know her and what makes her tick, has my body buzzing to touch and be near her, even when I should be pushing her the other way.

When our mouths touch and my tongue slides between her lips, my body reacts in a way I haven't felt in ages. This feeling is giving me a high—one that I don't want to come down from anytime soon. Her body against mine is making my cock unbearably hard, and every time a moan slips from her delicate lips, I want to push her legs apart and sink deep inside her.

Considering we're both completely naked in the creek and the sun is setting, I know I can't start anything we can't finish. Especially out here, but fuck do I want to. I want to so fucking badly that I have to talk myself down, so my body doesn't erupt before I even get the chance to feel how wet she is for me.

"Ah!" she squeals, pushing our bodies apart and twisting around. "I think something just touched me." She shifts her body, looking around as if it's going to jump out at her. "Are there alligators in here?" she asks, seriously.

Biting my lip, I try to stop the laughter that escapes my throat, but she hears it anyway.

"What?" She finally lifts her head.

I don't know how she hasn't noticed, perhaps my mouth was keeping her mind too occupied, but it definitely wasn't a creature in the water that touched her.

"Vada..." I say softly, reaching for her and pulling her back to my chest.

"No, I'm serious. I felt it."

"Felt it?" I quirk a brow. "Something like this?"

I push my hips into her until my cock brushes against the lower part of her stomach. "It was that snake you were talking about earlier..."

"Oh my God!" She bursts out laughing. Her eyes lower but between the darkness of the sky and the water, she can't see anything below my chest. "How's that even possible?"

"Well, it's not rocket science, sweetheart. Hot naked girl kissing me and rubbing her tits against me is going to make me hard." I shrug, unapologetically.

"Even in water?"

"Sweetheart, my cock's been hard since the moment you walked up my steps, and when you opened your smart mouth, it got even harder. So yes, *even* in water."

"Jesus," she whispers, pulling her bottom lip between her teeth as if she has to stop herself from saying anything else.

I align our bodies so we're facing each other and my cock

61

presses against her again. We lock eyes as I take one small step forward and feel my piercing rub against her clit. I hear a sharp inhale of breath as her shoulders tense, and her eyes flutter closed.

Palming my cock, I rub circles along her clit as she wraps her hands around my biceps, digging her nails into the muscle. Her breathing pattern quickens as I increase the pace, and when her head falls back, I know she's close.

"Does it feel this good when you touch yourself?" I ask roughly, wrapping my other hand around her neck and securing her body. I'm centimeters from being inside her, but I won't make the next move until she gives me permission. "Answer me, Vada."

"Fuck off," she finally responds, her eyelids barely open from the increased pressure.

"I know you're close," I say matter-of-factly. "So tell me," I demand, sliding my hand from her neck down to her breast and palming it with force. Squeezing her breast and rubbing her clit with my dick is going to unravel me any second, but I won't until I feel her body release.

"No!" she cries out, finally saying what I was hoping to hear.

"So you admit the real thing is better than doing it your-self?" I ask, rotating the tip of my cock the other direction as I feel her body tensing up.

"No," she grits between her teeth, stubbornly—not that I'm really surprised. It makes me smile still.

"No? So I should stop then and let you finish yourself?" I ask, slowing my rhythm, as painful as it is for me. I won't let her win this battle without a fight.

"Fuck, no!" Her eyes blink open in a panic as her chest rises and falls while she tries to catch her breath. "Okay, fine. Yes! Your stupid pierced cock feels fucking amazing against my clit. There! Happy?"

A smile shines over my face because I know how salty those words must've tasted coming out. "Extremely."

She groans, shifting her body so she can slide her hand between her legs. "I'm so close, I can finish myself anyway."

"Fuck that." I quickly grab her hands and wrap them around my waist, securing them with only one of my hands. "You change your answer yet?"

"I thought I did already," she hisses, wiggling her hips to find relief. My cock is still standing at attention, but I tilt my body just enough so it doesn't touch her.

"I need to hear you say it, Vada," I tell her seriously. "I'll fuck your cunt harder than you could ever imagine, but I won't until you know exactly what you're getting into."

She's breathing heavier now, and I can tell I have her full attention.

"And what is that?" she asks, panting.

"I'm not those guys in your romance novels. I'm a gentleman, and I'll treat you real good in bed, but I'm not one of those guys who sends flowers and chocolate the next day, so I don't want you getting the wrong idea here. You're tense as hell, and the only way to get you to relax is to fuck you so good, you'll still be feeling me days later."

"I have no expectations from you, Ethan," she tells me honestly. "I'm only here for a few more days, and then I'm gone."

"Good," I say, releasing my grip around her wrists. "Right

now, you should only concern yourself with how hard I can make you come, because sweetheart, after tonight your expectations are going to be a lot higher."

"Oh God," she whispers.

"So what's it going to be, Vada? Think one night with me will be enough for you?" I taunt, licking my lips as she looks up at me. Resisting the urge to kiss her, I wait impatiently for her response.

"I think the real question is...will one night with me be enough for *you*, Casanova?"

~

I nearly carry Vada back to the house, naked, but she makes me grab our clothes and get dressed before leading her the couple blocks back. I couldn't wait any longer. The way she makes me crave her is starting to become painful for my dick, and I know the only relief will come from her.

Wearing only my jeans, I rush us through the front door and immediately pin her against the door with my mouth. Before she can even finish moaning my name, my jeans are on the floor.

"I told you getting dressed was pointless," I say against her lips as I reach for her shirt and pull it over her head.

"You barely had any clothes on in the first place," she reminds me as I take her shorts off next. "I don't know if it's tradition to run naked outside in the south or something, but from where I'm from, public indecency gets you a misdemeanor."

"Good to know. Unshaved pussies should be fined," I tease,

kneeling down between her legs as she holds onto the door for support.

"Yeah? What about bad boys who watch their tenants masturbate? Is there a law against that?" she asks with a condescending tone as I slide her panties down to her ankles. Once she steps out of them, I fling them behind me.

Before answering, I grab her thighs and spread them. She squeals and rests her palms on my shoulders as she regains her balance. My mouth is on her before she can spit out another word.

Sliding my tongue along her slit, I circle her clit and taste all Vada's sweetness. She moans and digs her nails into my scalp as she pulls strands of my hair between her fingers.

Her body shakes as I sink my tongue deep inside her. She tastes so fucking good, I can't pull myself away.

"Holy fuck, Ethan..." she mutters, her hands roughly pulling at my hair, which feels surprisingly amazing when my mouth is on her.

My tongue devours her, sliding up and down her slit, sucking hard on her clit, and when I feel her body start to tense, I insert a finger inside her tight cunt.

"Oh my God," she says between gritted teeth, trying to keep herself together, but I know it's no use. She's going to unravel at any moment.

Speeding up the pace, I add a second finger as my tongue circles her clit faster. Her knees are seconds from buckling, and when she screams out my name, I push my fingers inside even deeper.

"Mm..." I groan against her pussy. Fuck, she tastes amazing. She's panting as I lick and clean her up, wanting to savor everything she gives me. Standing, I wrap my hand around her neck and without another word, pull her mouth to mine. She's reluctant at first, but it only takes her seconds to relax against me.

"Never tasted your own come before?" I pull back and ask. She licks her lips, and her eyes slowly trail up to mine, embarrassed by my question.

"I don't make it a habit."

I chuckle, figuring that's a no. "You should," I tell her. "Tastes like heaven, don't you think?" I smirk, brushing my tongue along my bottom lip.

She grinds her teeth down. "I wouldn't know. Guess I'll have to take your word for it."

"Smart girl." I wink. "Come on." I grab her hand before she can speak and lead her upstairs. We round the banister, and I walk us to the last door on the left.

Once we're inside, I shut the door behind us, and when she turns to face me, I know something's wrong.

"This is your room?" She raises her brows as she looks around the nearly empty space.

"No," I say, firmly. "I told you. No pussies in my bed except for Wilma."

"Oh, didn't realize you were serious."

"I'm always serious when it comes to pussy, Vada." I step closer, wrapping my hands around her and unhooking her bra. We both watch as it slides down her arms and falls to the floor. "You can change your mind, you know?" I reassure her, feeling uneasy about her mood shift.

"You don't sleep with women in your bed?"

"No."

"Why?"

I wrap my hand around my neck and squeeze. "That's not something I talk about. With anyone."

"So it's really just about the sex then?"

"Yes," I answer honestly. "That's all this is Vada. Can you handle that?"

"I already said yes," she reminds me, but she doesn't sound as certain as before.

"Good, because after tasting you once, I know I'm going to want to taste you again."

She looks up at me with wide eyes and smiles. I can tell her sex life was merely nonexistent before, which in a way makes me glad because I want to be the one to introduce her to all the amazing different ways I can make her feel fucking fantastic.

"So tell me what you like." I step forward, closing the gap between us. Wrapping my hand around her waist, I pull us chest to chest.

"What?"

"You write about sex for a living. You must have a preference."

"Uh…"

I smile, seeing the blush creep up her neck and cheeks. "How about this? If you're uncomfortable with anything I'm doing, you tell me, and I'll stop."

"Like a safe word?"

Chuckling, I say, "Sure. Is that what your characters do?"

She shrugs, her cheeks turning redder. "Sometimes."

"Okay. What's your safe word then?"

She chews the inside of her cheek as if she's really thinking about it. My cock is pressed against her stomach and the longer she takes, the more it aches.

"How about Henry?" she finally blurts out.

I blink. "Henry?"

"Yup."

"Big cock pun." I arch a brow, squeezing my fingers into her hip.

"I was thinking more along the lines of 'terrifying cock who chases after me,' but either one works." She's smiling and holding back laughter and fuck it's so goddamn adorable. If she wasn't standing in front of me completely naked, all wet with perky tits, I'd find all this talking before extremely annoying, but for some reason, it's not with her.

"Okay, so we're good now? You have your safe word, all the expectations are laid out, and my dick is rock hard and going to bust if you don't let me kiss you soon."

A smirk forms on her face as she grinds her body against my cock. "And who said chivalry was dead?"

I grin. "Probably a romance writer."

CHAPTER NINE

VADA

THE WORDS all but leave his lips before his mouth is back on mine. I take everything he gives me—his tongue, his hands, his body. I want it all. Even if it's temporary—a quick fix—I want it. I want *him*.

His touch consumes me, taking away my breath all in one motion. He palms my ass cheeks and lifts me up until my legs instinctively wrap around his waist. Feeling his erection against my leg, I rock my hips against him until I feel the tip of his cock against my clit. His piercing is giving me all kinds of curious and naughty thoughts.

"Vada, *fuck*," he growls against my ear. "Any time you do that, I want to bend you over and fuck that tight little ass."

I swallow, rotating my hips once again. "Would this be the appropriate time to say, *Henry*?" I joke, knowing that even if I wanted to use our safe word, I wouldn't unless I truly meant it.

"Oh, sweetheart," he drawls, walking us to the bed, "I haven't even started to make you question your decision to be with me yet. At least wait out the good stuff." He winks, laying me down once we reach the mattress.

"I've been questioning my decisions since the moment you opened the door."

He towers over my body with his hands firmly planted on both sides of me. Leaning down just enough to brush his lips against mine again with my legs still wrapped around his waist, he whispers, "It's freeing, isn't it? Once you stop overthinking and analyzing every little thing, you start learning how to have fun again."

"I think it's safe to say I haven't been thinking straight since I got here," I admit.

"So why start now?" He flashes his infamous panty-melting smirk that keeps me hypnotized.

I roll my eyes playfully, agreeing that being with him would indeed be freeing. Maybe even a little careless.

"So you're saying if I have sex with you, I'll magically get over my writer's block and finish my manuscript?" I tease, although the thought is intriguing.

"Baby, you have sex with me, and you won't be able to type fast enough." He feathers his kisses down my jawline and neck, landing on my earlobe.

My hair cascades around me as I laugh at his overconfidence. Although I have *zero* doubt the man's performance will be nothing short of amazing, I have to remind myself that this thing between us can only be physical.

"Sounds like a T-shirt slogan. *Have sex with Ethan Rochester and never have writer's block again!* You'd have a line of women around the block."

He lifts his head, the corner of his mouth tilts up as if he's giving it some real thought. "You willing to give me an editorial review? You know, to put on the website and all."

"You wouldn't need a review. Just a picture of your abs and python-sized cock, and they'd be running over each other faster than a sale on Black Friday."

"Okay, now you're just making me sound like a piece of meat. I have feelings, you know."

"There's no feelings in fucking," I remind him, although I'm the one who needs convincing.

"Fuck," he growls, the tip of his cock torturously brushing against my clit again as he roughly palms my breast. "I think that's the hottest thing I've ever heard a woman say."

"Yeah? Well, show me like you mean it then," I challenge, arching my hips because the way he's taunting me drives my body insane. His piercing rubs against my pussy again, and I'm two seconds away from flipping him over and riding him like the Raging Bull roller coaster at Six Flags—*hard and fast*.

He leans back briefly, reaching into the nightstand near the bed and opens the drawer. At first, I'm confused, but then I see he pulls out a strip of condoms. Jesus, does he buy them in bulk? Or perhaps he should just buy stock in the damn things. *He probably already does.*

He tears one off but doesn't open it. I watch as he kneels down between my legs and without saying another word, grabs my thighs and pushes my knees to my shoulders.

"Ah!" I yelp, surprised by his quick movements. My ass is hanging off the edge of the bed as he kneels on the floor and presses his mouth directly on my clit.

The moment his tongue sinks inside me, I feel my body floating. His hands palm my ass cheeks as he devours me like the starved man he is. He moans in pleasure as he licks up and down my slit, bringing me closer to the edge with every calculated movement.

"Holy fuck, Ethan," I blurt out, my head falling back as I arch my body and his tongue slides in deeper. My nails dig into the sheets, and I'm clawing at them with every long stroke he gives me. The way he rotates the tip of his tongue has me moaning and screaming, both wanting more and needing the release.

His mouth takes no prisoners.

A finger slides inside, and he fucks me as he tastes my arousal. I'm so close, but the moment I'm about to come, he teases me with another finger. I'm ready. I need it so fucking badly, and just as my body tightens, he slips one of his fingers into my tight ass.

"Oh my God!" I squeal, my nails digging deeper into the mattress.

It's so unexpected, and the feeling is so foreign, yet the moment my body relaxes, I know I've never come that hard from oral before.

"Hurts good, doesn't it, sweetheart?" Ethan towers over me, drinking me in as my eyelids flutter open.

It takes me a few moments to catch my breath, and while I do, he kisses my neck, shoulder, and chest. He wraps his lips around my nipple and playfully flicks it before moving onto the other.

"Now I see I was right about you..." I give him a dreamy look that proves just how completely smitten I am by him. Even before I saw the whole package, I knew there was something about him. Something *mysterious*.

"And what's that, darlin'?" He muses.

"That you're a bad boy," I tell him, at the same time reminding myself, *Don't get attached. Just sex.*

His smile deepens, and I know it's not because he finds me funny.

"Baby, I'm not a bad boy." His tone is steady and honest, and although I want to believe that with every beat of my heart, deep down I know otherwise.

I pluck my bottom lip between my teeth as I gaze up and study him.

"Maybe not, but you're definitely bad for me."

Without saying another word, he steps back and sheaths his cock before pressing his tip against my entrance.

"You still sure then?" he asks, wrapping a hand around my neck, so our mouths are only inches apart.

Swallowing, I nod. "Yes."

He slides into me in one smooth motion before sliding back out. God, he's so thick. His piercing rubs along my walls and brings an added sensation all together. I kind of like it.

As he presses our mouths together, he pushes back in, this time rocking his hips back and forth. My legs are tightly holding him against my body as if he'll get away. I want him. I *need* him. Everything he's giving me, *anything*, I'll take it.

"Fuck, you feel so good, Vada," he whispers, wrapping a fist in my hair and pulling. "Who knew a big-mouthed city girl would have such a tight little cunt?"

His words are so crass, yet my body gets hotter every time I hear him talk like that. The characters in my books aren't any better, but I never realized the words sounded as good on paper as they do in real life.

"You like when I talk like that?" he asks. When I don't respond, he continues, "I felt you tighten when I talked about your cunt. You liked it, didn't you?"

"I write about cunts and cocks all the time," I blurt out like it's an excuse for my body's response.

His brow arches, amused. "Well, I hope you're taking some good notes, baby. I'm about to show you just how bad I can be."

Before I can truly comprehend his words, he steps back, grabs my ankles from around his waist and places them on top of his shoulders. He nearly bends me in half when he leans back over my chest and roughly pushes inside.

"Shit," I curse, as I suck in a deep breath. "This sounds a lot easier in books."

"Not as flexible as your characters?" He winks, driving his cock in deeper.

"Not when I spend the majority of my time on my ass."

"Or back," he counters.

The laughter that releases is hijacked by a deep moan. He increases his pace, wraps his hand around my neck again, and pulls my face closer to his.

"I want you to watch, Vada. Watch my cock sliding inside you. Watch me fucking you because sweetheart, it's the hottest fucking thing I've seen in a long time."

Straining my neck to see where our bodies connect, I watch as he slowly pulls out—so slow it's torturous. His piercing pushes against the latex, and just as I'm about to beg him to take me out of my misery, he forcefully pushes back inside me.

"Ah, God!" My head starts to fall back in pleasure, but Ethan grips me harder.

74

"No. Watch," he demands.

Blinking, I do.

Fuck, it's so hot. I've written several sex scenes over the years, yet I've never actually watched with intention.

"See how our bodies stay in sync?" His eyes lower. "Like they were made to fuck each other."

"Wow…real Shakespeare shit right there," I tease, getting antsy because I need to come again. Just when I feel the orgasm building, he slows his pace.

"I'm a man of many qualities." He grins.

"I have no doubt."

"You need to come," he says—not a question.

I nod, eagerly.

"Show me how you rub your clit," he orders.

"Watching me once wasn't enough for you?" I fire back.

"I could watch you every day and never get bored. Rub your clit until you come. I want to watch you while I fuck you."

My cheeks redden at the memory of him seeing me. I know I shouldn't be embarrassed, but I can't help it, especially since his abs were the reason I came as hard as I did that night.

Obeying him, I slide my hand between us and circle my clit. His grip around my neck relaxes as the pressure builds.

"Jesus Christ. You squeeze my dick so fucking hard when you get close."

"I know." I smile. I have way more experience getting myself off than I care to admit. Trust issues, failed dating attempts, and lack of social skills is to blame.

"Open your eyes. Watch our bodies as you come."

"I don't think I can," I say, breathlessly. My fingers circle my clit faster and harder, and soon it's all too much to bare.

"Vada!" he growls, grabbing my attention. My eyes shoot open, and as soon as I see his intent stare, my body unravels.

He slows his pace as I ride out the wave, my hand falling slack against the mattress. My chest rises and falls as I feel him slide all the way out.

"I won't be surprised if I'm missing a layer of skin tomorrow," Ethan teases. "Your pussy's so fucking hungry."

Yeah, it's been a while. Tell me something I don't know. I roll my eyes at myself, not saying the words aloud.

"I'm not done with you yet." His words vibrate against the shell of my ear, and soon I'm being lifted into the air and flipped onto my stomach. "Ass up."

"My entire body is jelly," I try to explain, but when he slides his hand up my spine, I push my ass out for him.

"I warned you," he growls. "There's no way I'm fucking you without getting an ass view."

"You warned me?" I question, putting my body into position so I can rest my head on the mattress while my ass is in the air, patiently waiting.

"I knew you were tense as hell, and the only way you'd relax was to fuck you so good, you'd be feeling me days later," he reminds me, repeating what he told me almost word for word.

"Right," I murmur to myself, but by the way he positions his cock against my pussy, I know he heard me.

"I think it's safe to say you're pretty relaxed now, but just in case, I plan to fuck you until we're both raw and bruised."

Raw and bruised? What does this man have planned for me? I wondered but didn't have time to dwell on it before his length was deep inside me.

My fingers dig into the sheets as he palms my ass cheeks and spreads them apart. He squeezes my hips and pushes me harder and faster into him as he speeds up his own pace.

"Fuck...fuck..." I moan, closing my eyes tightly as I take every brutal thrust. One of his hands release me, but within seconds, I feel it smack against my ass cheek. "Ah!" I yelp, jerking forward.

"That's for teasing me with this ass since the second you got here." He does it again and once more before tightening his grip on my hip and fucking me so hard, I fear I might break.

I smile although he can't see me, knowing that he's been lusting over me since the moment we met.

"Goddammit, Vada..." he hisses, anger and lust woven into his tone. "You feel too fucking good." Releasing his hold on me, he leans his body over my back and snakes a hand over my breast, squeezing roughly. I've always liked my breasts touched and played with, but by the way Ethan is handling them, you'd think they'd done him wrong in some way.

His hand slides down my stomach and lands on my pussy. Arching my back more, his cock moves in deeper while the pad of his finger rubs my clit.

"I love how tense you get before you come," he whispers into my ear. "Then a second before you do, your body relaxes, and you release everything out of your mind. For a moment, you have no thoughts, no concerns, no worries. It's pure fucking bliss."

"Yes," I moan in agreement. "Coming is the best high there is."

"Then I better make sure it's worth your while, huh?" His

lips smile against my neck. "Your pussy is like heaven. I never want to vacate."

"Sorry, one-night stay per guest only." I grin.

"Fuck that," he growls, adding more pressure to my clit as he speeds up his pace. "The only guest allowed to check-in is my dick, sweetheart."

"Who knew you were so territorial?" I mock, knowing he hasn't been up to this point.

"Not me. Definitely not me," he says as if he's shocked by his own words. "However, that was before your cunt took over my brain."

Before I get the chance to make another joke about his southern charm, my body goes rigid, and his fingers continuously rub my clit as my body tightens all around him. Seconds later, he goes still, and I know he's not far behind.

Leaning back, he grabs my hips roughly and our bodies rock together. Our skin smacks together so hard and fast, I can barely keep up.

"Fuck, fuck, fuck," he hisses on a moan as he stills, our bodies shaking together as he releases inside me.

He groans as he pushes once more against me and curses. "Shit, Vada."

My entire body goes lax. I can't feel my arms or legs. Before sliding out and tossing the condom, he leans over me and presses a sweet kiss against my neck.

I flip over and settle into the bed, enjoying the warmth. Although the room is dark, there's a flicker of light coming from the moon outside the window. It glows against his tan skin, insinuating every part of him that was just mine. Stunning and beautiful, I can almost see right through him and the facade he hides behind.

"Mission accomplished," he says as he lies next to me in bed.

"Mission?" My brows arch. "I was a mission?"

"Rode my dick raw and yet...I want more." He turns and looks at me, waiting for my reaction.

I'm not quite sure how to react, but I smile in agreement.

"Yeah, I could get used to this," I say, dreamily. "Although, it feels like my pussy needs an ice pack and a cigarette." I squeeze my eyes shut the moment the words spew from my lips. "These scenes are way sexier in romance novels."

He chuckles, pulling the blankets that survived and covers us up. Even though I know he's not the flowers and chocolates kind of guy, I'm hoping this doesn't make things weird between us. I still have four days here, and if we can stick to the sexual stuff only, this will be the best writer's retreat of my life.

CHAPTER TEN

ETHAN

I HAVEN'T SLEPT with a woman since Alana. I've had plenty of one-night stands, but sleepovers weren't a thing I allowed. At least not until right now.

Having Vada sleeping against my chest feels intimate, yet I'm not pushing her away like I should—like I usually do. Her body heat feels nice, and for the first time, I'm not going to bed feeling empty and alone.

Even if that's exactly how I wanted it all these years.

Closing my eyes, flashes of Alana and the memory of the life we shared evades my mind. I manage to get a few hours' sleep before those memories wake me.

After a half hour of watching Vada sleep next to me, I decide to stop fighting it and get out of bed. I slide on my shorts, and before leaving the guest bedroom, I turn around and stare at her. I don't know what comes over me, but I walk to her side of the bed, pull off the covers, and wrap her in my arms. As quietly as I can, I carry her out of the room and walk us to my bedroom where I lay her down and cover her back up. She looks good in here. Looks right.

And that scares the shit out of me.

The guest room is the only bed I've let women be with me in, and the status of being a one-night only hookup doesn't fit right with Vada. I know I've set the rules for us, and we both know what to expect of this, but our connection isn't on the same level as a random one-night stand. Leaving her in there just didn't feel right.

Once I'm in the hallway, I shut the door and tiptoe down the stairs. I decide to make a pot of coffee since I know sleep won't be coming to me anytime soon.

After filling up my mug, I head upstairs and go to the tower. The sun should be rising shortly, and the tower has a perfect view of it.

Memories of Alana and I first looking at this house comes to mind. We met in a small town, high school sweethearts you could say, and were each other's firsts. Everyone expected us to get married, have kids, and live happily ever after.

Too bad life had other plans for us.

After living the apartment life for two years, we decided it was time to start house hunting. It just so happened we found the right one at just the right time. Alana was six months pregnant when we found our house.

"Babe, come check the view from up here!" she called from the third story when I was still climbing the stairs to the second floor. It was a traditional southern house with original wood, wraparound porch with three-bedrooms and two point five bathrooms. It even had a big yard, which was something we both wanted.

"Coming, hold on," I called back. "How'd you get up there so fast?"

Alana might've been pregnant, but she didn't let that stop her. She was as active as she'd always been. Both in and out of the bedroom.

"This is the part of the house I wanted to see the most. It's amazing," she said with adoration in her voice.

I finally caught up to her, taking the final steps into the tower. Windows surrounded it in a complete three-hundred-and-sixty-degree view. You could see for miles up here.

"Wow," I said as I wrapped my arms around her waist from behind. She covered my hands with hers as we stood in the middle of the tower and just stared out.

"I know," she whispered. "Imagine all the sunrises and sunsets we could watch from up here."

"And fireworks over the water," I added. "It's perfect."

"It's like being on the Eiffel Tower." She beamed, and I knew no other house would even come close to this one. Alana had been obsessed with the Eiffel Tower since our honeymoon when we visited a couple years ago. The beauty of it inspired her to focus more on what made her happy.

"I could do all my pottery up here," she told me as we both glanced around the space. "Put my wheel in the middle, my wood shelves along that wall over there for all my mugs, and put the kiln on the other wall. What do you think?" She looked over her shoulder at me with pleading eyes. Alana loved pottery, and even more, loved creating it. I couldn't deny her of what made her truly happy, especially if it meant I got to see that beautiful smile every day.

"I think you're absolutely right. The space is perfect for it, and you really can't beat the view." I gave her a tight squeeze for emphasis. "You think you'll still have time after the baby arrives?"

"Probably not at first, but eventually when we have a schedule down," she explained, and I agreed.

"Good." I kissed the top of her head. "You're too talented not to."

"If you don't buy me this house, I'll divorce you," she teased with a laugh.

"It's pretty perfect," I agreed. I turned her around and knelt down. Rubbing a hand over her belly, I spoke softly, "What do you think, Paris? Do you want this to be your first home?" I looked up at Alana, smiling down at me as I talked to our daughter.

Seconds later, she kicked.

And that was all the confirmation we needed.

We put in an offer, and a month later, we moved in. I'd spent the following few weeks finishing up the nursery, knowing Alana wanted it perfect. The house needed some updating, but I knew we'd have to do a little here and there until it was complete. It was something we were supposed to do together.

At thirty-two weeks, Alana went into early labor and had no choice but to deliver. She was preeclamptic, and the doctor didn't want to risk waiting longer. As much as we were excited to finally be meeting our little girl, I was also scared. Becoming a father for the first time is something I've been thinking about for years. Especially with Alana.

Everything started out smoothly as they induced Alana, and it became a waiting game as she started getting contractions. The doctor warned us it could be awhile before she'd be ready to push, so in attempt to keep her distracted, we talked about all the remodeling plans we had for the new house.

The next several hours were spent getting Alana ice, rubbing her back and shoulders, and massaging her feet. The contractions became more intense and closer together. She was tough, always had been, and even though she wanted to have a natural birth as much as possible, she started to beg for an epidural.

"Alana," I said softly. "You're doing great, baby. Are you sure you want the epidural?" I asked because she had made me promise to not let her get one, even though I didn't see any reason not to when she was in this much pain.

"I can't bare the pain, E. It's like she's clawing her way out," she cried, and I winced. I couldn't stand watching her suffer any longer.

"Okay, baby." I grabbed her hand and kissed it. "I'll tell the doctor."

"Ah!" she screamed out and clenched my fingers in a forceful fist. She squeezed her eyes and lips, and I knew something was wrong.

I paged the nurse, and shortly after she came back in the room, she checked all of Alana's stats on the monitor and read the contractions record. The baby monitor that wrapped around her belly had shifted slightly.

Once the nurse retightened the strap and the stats flashed on the screen, a look of worry flashed across her face.

"Is everything okay?" I asked, concerned.

"The baby's heartbeat is slower than I'd like, so I'm just going to page the doctor and have him come check you out."

She rushed out before I could ask more questions.

"Is the baby going to be okay?" Alana's eyes watered, and I knew I had to keep her calm.

"I'm sure it's nothing, but the doctor will come and check," I reassured her, but I wasn't certain myself.

Within a few minutes, the doctor had arrived and checked hers and the baby's stats again. Two nurses followed.

"Alana, we're going to roll you to your side and see if that helps increase the heartbeat. Okay?"

The nurses helped Alana get comfortable on her side, and after a moment, the heart rate went back up.

"Perfect." The doctor smiled.

"Is she okay?" Alana asked.

"She is for now, but if the heart rate drops again, we'll have to deliver via C-section."

"What? Why?" Alana cried, looking panicked.

"Vaginal delivery is too risky if the baby is in distress. Her heart rate decreasing during birth could put her at risk for too many complications, and I'd like to avoid all that." His words come out rehearsed, and I wish he'd give us some closure that everything was going to be okay.

We waited an hour before the doctor returned and told us the bad news.

"I'm sorry, the heart rate isn't staying as steady as much as I'd like. I'd feel more confident if we did a C-section to avoid any other risks."

Since she was preeclamptic, she was already a high-risk case, so we had no choice but to follow the doctor's orders.

Everything happened so fast after that. The nurses prepped Alana for surgery, and I changed into scrubs. They gave us a briefing of what to expect, but no matter what they told us, none of it felt real.

They took Alana in first, and once the doctor was ready, the nurse escorted me inside by her.

"Baby," I whispered, kissing her cheek. She looked terrified and as scared as I was, I couldn't let her see that.

"E," she whispered back. "Please tell me she's going to be okay."

I kissed her again. "Everything's going to be fine. I promise, okay?"

I flashed her a smile. I couldn't see much over the sheet they put between Alana and the doctor, but I could tell she felt some discomfort.

"You okay?"

"I can feel pressure, that's all. It feels weird."

"Well, in just a minute, we're going to have a daughter. Can you believe it?" I smiled so wide as I held her hand.

"Okay, Mom and Dad. Are you ready?" the doctor announced. I was anxious but so excited to meet my daughter. "Here she is." He lifted her up briefly giving us just a peek at her. "She's beautiful, congratulations," he said after handing her off to one of the nurses.

"Oh my God," Alana cried. I knew she was upset about not having a natural delivery, but having my two girls healthy and safe was the most important thing.

"She looks just like you," I said. "So beautiful." I kissed her softly on the lips. "Thank you."

Tears poured from her eyes and fell down her face. "For what?"

"For the greatest gift you could've ever given me."

I kissed her again.

"Can you go with her? She's going to be in the NICU, and I don't want her to be alone."

"I don't want to leave you, baby..." I was so damn torn. I needed to make sure Paris was okay, but at the same time, it felt like I was abandoning Alana.

"I'll be okay," she promised with a hand squeeze. "They have to finish putting my stomach back together and then set me up in a room anyway."

"Are you sure?" I looked around the room as the doctor continued working on Alana and the nurses tended to Paris.

"Yes. Go, please!"

I kissed her once more. "I love you, baby. I'll get an update on Paris as soon as I can, okay?"

"I love you, too, E." She smiled up at me, and we both stared into each other's eyes as I walked toward the nurses.

They cleaned Paris and were preparing to transfer her. She looked so small in the incubator, and I still couldn't believe she was ours.

"Is she okay?" I asked a nurse who was looking at her chart.

"Her breathing is unsteady, and she looks jaundiced, but everything else looks okay so far." She smiled up at me. "They'll take good care of her up in the NICU. Don't worry."

"Thank you."

Another nurse introduced herself as she arrived and explained she'd be the one bringing Paris down to the NICU. I followed her as she wheeled the little cart to the elevator and took us to the fifth floor. I wasn't prepared. I wasn't prepared for any of this, and I felt like a damn fool.

As we walked the quiet path down the hallway, I could see in the other rooms. Tiny, helpless babies all in incubators. I'd never witnessed anything like it in my life.

I was anxious to get back to Alana, but I knew she'd want me to stay with Paris until I had a solid update. My baby girl was covered in tubes. A breathing tube and feeding tube, along with a variety of monitors.

The scene broke me.

I felt incredibly helpless as I watched our newborn baby fighting to breathe. She was premature, weighing only four pounds, and I wanted nothing more than for her to stay strong and healthy.

About an hour later, the doctor who did Alana's C-section knocked on the door, and as soon as I saw his glum expression, I stood from my chair and walked toward him.

I waited for him to speak, but his eyes flickered to Paris and back to mine before he finally did.

"There were some complications with Alana," he began, and I felt my entire world ripped out from under me.

Those memories continue to haunt me in every aspect of my life. I blamed and beat myself over not being there for her when she needed me the most—completely vulnerable and exposed. To have to choose between being by my wife's side or my newborn baby was a game I couldn't win. I'd already felt guilty for leaving her in the operating room, but either choice would've been the wrong one. That's something I know I'll have to live with the rest of my life.

Just when I thought things couldn't get worse, after planning my wife's funeral and burying her, I watched helplessly as my baby girl fought for her life. Two weeks after I lost Alana, I lost Paris, too. She was too little, too sick, and I was heartbroken all over again.

I lost more than my wife and daughter—I'd also lost myself—and it's prevented me from ever wanting to fall in love again. At first, it was acceptable to grieve the way I did. I shut down, unable to step into the tower surrounded by her pottery and things, but when I heard a mouse up there one night, I went into a blind rage.

Being around her things that were left as if she were coming back to me, set me off. It mocked me, taunting me of everything I'd lost. All her clay and supplies. Her bowls and mugs. The old radio we bought at a rummage sale she'd play while working. The room still smelled like her.

The mouse squeaked as it ran across the room toward the other end, stealing my attention. Without thinking, I grabbed one of the empty buckets and threw it in his direction. I knew I'd miss, but the moment I released my grip, anger filled my body.

I grabbed the next bucket and threw that, too. Then another. Picking up and throwing anything I could get my hands on. For a solid minute, I destroyed everything in my way. By the time I stopped, I was out of breath and silently cursing myself. But releasing the anger felt necessary and overdue.

Aunt Millie found me sitting in the tower the next morning. She could see the mess I'd created and that I was self-destructing. She knew how much Alana meant to me and how her unexpected death derailed me.

"Ethan, hon, I know you're hurting. You have every right to be, but this isn't the man Alana would want you to be." Her voice was soft, but firm.

"What's it matter, Aunt Millie? My life is over. It's nothing without her."

"I know it feels that way right now, but you need to grieve and give yourself permission to move on and be happy again. Alana would want you to," she told me, although I've heard it all before. It'd be two years since her death and no matter what people said, time didn't heal all wounds. Not at fucking all.

"I'll never be able to move on from this," I said, confidently. "I lost my family, my entire world, and my only reason for living."

"Find a way to connect with her, Ethan. Instead of thinking about everything you lost, find a way to keep her spirit alive within you." Her words were wise, and I appreciated them, but it wouldn't change anything. She'd still be gone.

"How?" I asked, defeated. Exhaustion was setting in, and nothing made sense.

"Find something she loved," she began, waving her hand around the mess I made and continuing, *"like pottery."*

"I can't make what she did, Aunt Millie. Even if I did, it was her dream. It'd feel as if I were taking it away from her." Emotions filled my throat, and I swallowed down a sob. I'd never felt that vulnerable in my life, and there I was sitting on the floor of the tower, my wife's favorite place, surrounded by the destruction I created.

"Quite the opposite." She patted my leg, sympathetically. *"You'll feel what she felt while she was creating her bowls and cups and connect with her through that. It could help give you closure, even if right now it feels like you'll never get it."*

The only closure I could ever feel was knowing that Alana wasn't alone. She and Paris had each other, and until I'd see them again, I'd be dead inside.

"Healing is a process, and it takes time, but that doesn't mean you stop living in the meantime." I knew she was trying to comfort me, but I felt too empty inside to take her words to heart. I didn't want to heal. Pain was the only comfort I had anymore. Pain was the only emotion I felt.

"I don't know how to live without her," I explained. *"It still feels like it all happened yesterday."*

"Try it, honey." She handed me a block of clay from the ground that was a victim of the destruction. *"You don't know till you try."*

Aunt Millie's words repeated in my head for weeks after that. I knew my family was still worried sick about me, but depression sucked me into its black hole, and I wasn't looking for a way out.

That'd been my life for years.

Then came the anniversaries and birthdays.

Those days I ended up blacking out completely. I couldn't bare the pain anymore, so I drank until I was numb.

Until I picked up that block of clay. It was like Alana was saving me from myself, from the personal hell I created. Somehow, she was still here with me, helping me get through the hard times just as she always did over the years. Learning her craft was hard, and I was terrible. Each day I made lopsided mugs and crooked sculptures, I wanted to quit but didn't. It was almost as if Alana was pushing me to create, to live out the dream she always wanted for us. That day, I promised myself I'd never let her down. So I worked harder, hoping she'd be watching me from heaven with our baby girl in her arms.

Aunt Millie was right after all—this time.

I smile now when I think about Alana and the memories we shared all those years together. Though I'm completely disinterested in relationships in general, Aunt Millie likes to remind me of Alana and how she'd want me to be happy, even if that meant moving on. I've had no interest in anything more than a one-night stand or random fling, but for the first time in a long while, the woman sleeping in my bed right now has me rethinking everything.

The thoughts in my head take me off guard, though I can't deny they're true. Vada came barreling into my life, so unexpected, and yet, it's as if I'd been waiting for her all this time.

These feelings scare the shit out of me because this all happened so quickly, but knowing she's leaving in a few days has my mind spinning. I want to make the most out of our time together, but I can't stop the guilt that continues to eat at me every time I look down at my left hand and see the ghost of the wedding ring I once wore.

CHAPTER ELEVEN

VADA

WAKING up with my body against hard muscles shocks the shit out of me. Making sure I'm not still dreaming, I slowly peel open my eyes. I don't recognize the room as the sun peeks through the windows, but I can tell it's early morning. This isn't the same room we started in last night. But I don't have much time to analyze it because when memories start flooding in, my cheeks heat. All the things he did to me, all the *ways* he molded my body, and the way I responded to them. *Holy shit. Yes*, we did that. *No*, I don't have any regrets.

Nerves take over as I think about sneaking out and doing the walk of shame. I haven't had to face a one-night stand since my early college days, so I feel completely disoriented. It's not like I can just leave and avoid him anyway, but the anxiety of facing him has me overthinking everything.

However, the weight of Ethan's bicep holds me in place. There's no way I can slip out of bed without waking him. As if he heard my thoughts, he hums against the shell of my ear and pulls me closer to him until my back presses against his warm, hard chest. Our bodies fit together like two jagged pieces of a puzzle that somehow line up perfectly. We both have our sharp edges, but somehow it works. His strong arms hold me like I'm his, and I can't help but smile at the fantasy of it all—because that's what it is—make believe. We've both agreed that this isn't anything more than sex and a good time.

Though I write sex scenes in descriptive detail in my novels, this morning, I have no words. That's something that doesn't happen often. Me, speechless? Yep. Being with him was exhilarating, to say the least. We're adults who are obviously missing something in our lives. Last night, Ethan made me realize exactly *what* I've been missing, unadulterated sex with no attachments.

One-night stands are not in my sexual repertoire. Too many times I've overly romanticized relationships, but the men I've dated were basically worthless, so there's that. No man has been able to live up to the expectations as the ones I write— alpha males, smart, loyal, *perfect*. After all my failed relationships, I'm fairly certain my perfect real-life hero doesn't exist, and if he does, I'm sure he's taken.

"Morning," Ethan says in a husky, deep tone against the crook of my neck. Goose bumps travel along my skin as he slides his hand across my bare stomach. I turn my head as his honey-colored eyes flutter open.

"Morning," I say, happy it's not as awkward as I imagined it'd be. Then again, knowing this is purely physical without any strings attached helps. I can open my heart for a few days then seal it back tight before I get back to Chicago as if nothing ever happened. My secret will stay in South Carolina, and Ethan will be my perfect sexspiration.

"Coffee?" I ask, ready to get my day started. Just as I scoot away from him to place my feet on the ground, he pulls me back to face him.

"Not so fast," he says with a sexy smirk on his lips.

My heart feels as if it will beat right out of my chest. Ethan rolls over, his face hovering above mine.

"Don't think I'm going to stop giving you shit just because I fucked your brains out." He winks, and I know for certain nothing has changed.

I laugh at his blunt confession and go along with it. "Honestly, I wouldn't expect anything less," I mock, just before he places a sweet, lingering kiss on my lips as his hand slides up my body and cups my breast. Folgers has nothing on Ethan Rochester. Morning sex is now the best part of waking up.

I sink into the taste of him, his hands exploring my body as our legs intertwine together and a noise from the hallway has us parting.

"Shit," he whispers.

He turns his body just as the door swings open. Scrambling, I quickly pull the sheet up to my chin as I stare at an older woman with salt and pepper hair, and a soft, sweet face. Her cheekbones are high, and I can tell she was really beautiful when she was younger, but time has been good to her. She makes eye contact with me then looks over at Ethan who gives no fucks that he's naked. The sheet covers the lower half of his body and instead of trying to hide from her, he places his hands behind his head.

"Well, good morning to you, too," he says to her with a sly

smile on his lips, and something about their expressions makes me think this isn't the first time this woman has caught him in bed with someone.

She crosses the room and smacks him across the head. "I know your mama taught you some manners. Now you gonna introduce us or what?"

My cheeks burn, and I'm shocked as she reaches her arm across Ethan's naked body to shake my hand.

"Honey, my name is Millie. I'm Ethan's favorite aunt."

"My only aunt." Ethan snorts.

I grab her hand in mine and shake it, making sure to keep my breasts covered. "I'm Vada."

"Well, it's nice to meet you, Vada. Sorry, my inconsiderate nephew forgot his manners this morning. Must have had a *late* night." She looks him up and down. "Get dressed. I'll meet you downstairs. Don't keep me waitin'."

Millie turns and gives me a sweet smile before leaving the room. I can hear the stairs creak with each step she takes.

"What the hell was that?" I ask with a nervous laugh, pulling the sheets tighter against my naked body.

He turns toward me and wraps an arm around my waist, pulling my body to his. "Sorry, that's Aunt Millie. She likes to come over unannounced sometimes. But usually there's not a woman in my bed, so I'm sure I'll have some explainin' to do." He grins, pressing a quick kiss against my cheek. "Get dressed and meet us downstairs. I'm pretty sure she'll be cooking something, and Aunt Millie doesn't like it when people let her food get cold. Don't get on her bad side this early in the day. She's a grudge holder." Ethan winks at me before slipping on a pair of jogging pants and leaving me alone in his room.

I sit quiet and still and can hear her muffled voice along with Ethan's. Scanning the room, I search for my clothes and remember they were in the other room. Wrapping the sheet around my body, I hurry down the hall, open the door and find them in a crumpled pile on the floor. I tiptoe across the worn wooden boards and glance over and see Wilma staring at me with her judgmental cat eyes. Each time I look at her, I think of my Oliver at home. He's a long-haired Siamese I rescued a few years ago. Most of the time, he's the only thing I talk to during the day. He's pretentious, but I think Wilma may have him beat on many other levels.

"Don't look at me like that," I whisper-hiss at her. "I'm not peeing on your territory."

Her tail flicks a few times before she turns around and prances down the stairs. I can hear the bell on her collar ring out, almost mocking me.

After I slip on my clothes, I find the bathroom and wash my face and freshen up. I'm sure more than enough time has passed beyond just getting dressed, but I try to work up the courage to face them both downstairs as if nothing happened between us. But considering his aunt now saw us naked in his bed, there's no story that can cover up what happened last night. Oh, God. I wrinkle my nose. *Does his room smell like sex and shame?*

I run my fingers through my hair until it's halfway work-able and throw it up into a messy knot before taking the stairs down and walking into the kitchen. Ethan's leaning against the counter showcasing his bare chest and hard muscles with a cup of coffee in his hand. His hair is a mess, but he easily swipes a hand through it, making it look as desirable as always. His lips move, flashing his perfect white teeth, and soon he's laughing at something and so is Millie.

"So, Vada," Millie drawls in a deeper accent than Ethan's. She pours coffee into one of his beautiful mugs and hands it to me. "Ethan tells me you're an author and write those romance books I like to read."

My cheeks heat and my eyes go wide. Met this woman ten minutes ago, naked in her nephew's bed, and now the only thing she knows about me is that I write steamy romance. Worst first impression ever.

"Actually, I told her you write smutty romance books," Ethan corrects with a grin. "But she knew what I was talking about. Millie's a dirty old woman, so don't let her sweet face and southern drawl fool you," he warns, teasing us both. "She probably even has one of those red rooms of pain in her house."

I narrow my eyes at him, and I'm halfway certain Millie is going to slap him upside the head again, but instead, she sets a plate in front of me with the breakfast works—bacon, eggs, and toast. Ethan sits next to me and smiles as Millie works around this kitchen like she owns the place, setting out salt, pepper, butter, and jelly in the middle of the table.

"I do like those romance books. An old woman like me can use as much loving she can get, even if it's through fiction. I love me some Danielle Steele and that E.L. James," she laughs, pretending to fan herself. "Ethan dear, you talk about the red room of pain as if you've read *Fifty Shades*."

He shuts up, which only causes me to burst into laughter.

"Did you really read it?" I ask, intrigued, and remember our safe word conversation from last night. He *totally* did.

"He likes to act like he's some hotshot, but I'm pretty sure I saw a few copies of it floating around the studio," Millie tells me matter-of-factly. "And, he has a *Fifty Shades of Grey* inspired mug, too."

"I was capitalizing, Aunt Millie. *Research.* And honestly, who hasn't read it? The FedEx guy told me he read it five times," he tells her, talking with his mouth full.

"Ethan Booker Rochester! I know your mama taught you better manners than talking with a mouth full of food." She scolds him like he's twelve, and it warms my heart that she doesn't take his shit either.

"Booker?" I arch a brow, teasingly.

"Family name," he explains, shrugging.

"Never would've taken you for a romance reader," I tease. "You seem more like the kind of guy who *prefers* pictures."

Millie smiles and sips her coffee, eyeing the two of us behind her mug. "So what's the story between you two anyway?"

I was waiting for her to ask. Actually, I'm surprised it took her this long. Curiosity fills her face, and I continue eating, focusing on my food, not really sure what to say.

"She's renting the cottage while she finishes her manuscript. Apparently, she's on a major deadline and came here for inspiration. I think she may have found it, Aunt Millie." Ethan pops an eyebrow up at me, and before I can even respond to his sexual innuendo, Millie continues with her questions.

"So you're one of Ethan's tenants?" Millie's trying to piece together the clues of why we were naked in bed this morning. She raises her eyebrows and waits for me to respond.

"Yes, that's correct." I clear my throat and speak up. "I'm from Chicago."

"Okay," she says, her smile not faltering a bit. "Well, you two look like you've hit it off pretty quick. Ethan is a good boy, though sometimes he can be...arrogant."

"Aunt Millie! I am most certainly *not*," Ethan protests as he laughs.

She playfully rolls her eyes at him. "You know, I don't like to use those swear words because it's not ladylike, but many people, especially those of the opposite sex, believe you are." She looks at me, then whispers, "The ladies are always chasing him, but he's too busy shooing them away."

"So you're gonna blast all my secrets to Vada, are you?" He pushes himself off the counter and pours himself more coffee. "I see how it's going to be."

Millie winks at me, and I can't help but smile as she removes my empty plate. I realize I do need to get to the cottage to write. My laptop is calling me, and inspiration is basically bursting from my fingertips. I'm still smiling thinking about all the words I'm about to write. I haven't felt this excited to work in weeks.

"I should probably get to the studio. I've got some things I need to take care of before lunch," Ethan says, giving Millie a sweet kiss on her cheek.

I stand, taking that as my cue to leave. "Thank you for breakfast. I really enjoyed it. It was nice to meet you."

"It was so nice meeting you, darling. Now, don't you be a stranger for the rest of the week. Remember to come out every once in a while to eat and give Ethan a dose of his own medicine." She walks over to me and opens her arms to pull me into a big hug. I'm not expecting this at all, so I awkwardly hug her back. Southerners—I seriously love their friendliness—but I'm not used to it. Before I head out, I grab my cup and refill it with coffee.

"Bye," I say with a small wave. "Thanks again for everything." I smile at Millie before glancing over at Ethan who's watching me with heat in his eyes.

His dark hair stacks on his head, and I have the urge to run my fingers through it. My body knows what it had and wants more—lots more. I swallow hard, a small smile playing on my lips as I replay last night before I turn around and leave.

Walking across the cobblestone that leads to the cottage, I hold my mug with a death grip and hope Ethan's huge cock doesn't come after me again. Just the thought makes me laugh.

I walk into the cottage and set my coffee down next to my closed laptop. I quickly change into something more comfortable and pull all my long hair up into a messy bun. Once I'm back in my writing uniform, I settle into the chair and prepare to kick my manuscript's ass.

After opening my laptop, I crack my fingers and read the last chapter I had written. Yesterday I struggled hard, and today I'm laughing at the cursor that's mocked me for the past few months.

As soon as my fingers hit the keys, the words fly out in sentences, paragraphs, then pages. Hours pass, and I can't seem to pull away from writing, not right now, when I'm pouring my heart and soul into the pages, but I know I need to take a break.

Considering I've been here for four days already, I know I need to call Nora and check on everything back home. It's been a while since I've left the house for longer than a weekend.

I stand up and stretch, allowing every vertebrae in my back to pop. That's when I realize how sore I actually am, and the only person to blame is Ethan. Pacing, trying to stretch my legs, I grab my phone and hit Nora's number.

The line rings over and over, and before I hang up, she picks up the phone.

"Hey, Nora," I say with a smile on my face, trying to be as friendly as possible because sometimes she can be a grump. But that's why I love her.

She groans then chuckles. "I was napping, Vada."

"At ten in the morning?" I know she's giving me shit, like usual.

"When you're retired, it's always nap time," she informs me. "So what can I help you with? And before you can even ask, the cat is still alive. I've been feeding him every day and following the psychotic instructions you left for me."

"Have you been giving him his treats? The beef ones in the plastic container by the coffee maker," I remind her for probably the fourth time. Oliver is particular with his treats and doesn't really care for the seafood ones. I'm pretty sure he can sniff out artificial fish flavor from a mile away.

"Yes, but he snubs me each time I walk in and realizes it isn't you. I'm pretty sure he hates me." I can hear Nora opening and closing cabinets. If I close my eyes, I can imagine her pulling one of her favorite mugs with some sarcastic saying on it from the cabinet and pouring a cup of coffee. When I hear her sip loudly, I know that's exactly what she was doing.

"He can just sense when an angry old lady walks into the room," I reply, trying to get a laugh from her.

"Oh, I'm sure he can." She groans. "What's up with you? You sound...*different*." She waits for me to speak, and I wonder if she can tell something's up. She's over thirty years older than me and has this crazy mother's intuition when it comes to my life. Though she's grumpy and sarcastic most of the time, I love her like a crazy aunt. When I'm lonely or need plot help, she listens and gives me advice when I need it. Now that I think about it, Nora may be my only friend at home. I really need to get out more.

"Uh..." I stare out the window toward the house and images of the night flash through my memory like photographs. "Actually," I begin, clearing my throat, "I had sex. And not just boring, old married couple missionary sex either. Really *good* sex."

"What? I didn't hear you. Old age, remember?" She snickers.

I roll my eyes and speak louder. "I had sex last night, and it was amazing."

"If I could figure out how to use this damn iPhone, I'd tell you to text me a picture of Mr. Wonderful."

I laugh. "He's actually the type I stay away from, which is shocking."

She knows exactly what type I'm talking about—that bad boy, I'll dump-you-in-a-day type.

"Ahh," is all she offers. Nora knows intricate details about my past relationships, why they didn't work out, and how I've been unable to have a long-term relationship in years.

"It's a no-strings attached kind of thing," I explain, and can just imagine her shaking her head in disdain, giving me that salty look she's known for before she breaks into a knowing smile.

"I'm sure it would have to be considering you're due home in three days, but you're young and beautiful. It's about time you had a little fun. Just make sure to leave your heart at the door or on the floor, well, unless you were on the floor." She pauses as I release a chuckle. "Anyway, you know what I mean. Just don't get hurt, kid. You know I kinda like you like the daughter I never had."

"Kinda? Well thanks, Nora. It's just some adult fun. I mean, what could really happen in three days?"

She laughs. "Ask Cinderella. And just to be clear, you're staying on deadline, right? If your agent found out you weren't writing and was…"

"Hardy har har," I say. "Yes, I'm on track. But speaking of, I need to get back to work. Thanks for taking care of Oliver. Kiss him for me."

She makes a noise. "Yuck. And get cat hair all over me? No, thank you. Keep me updated, and call me if you need anything, okay?"

"Thanks, Nora. I will." We hang up, and I immediately get back to work. I write until I've finished five more chapters — a new personal record that I couldn't be prouder of. Over eight thousand words have been added to my manuscript, and if I have a few more days like this, I'll finally be on schedule. But I'm trying not to jinx myself or creativity. I suck in a deep breath and look out the window and realize it's almost four in the afternoon. Though I want to keep writing, I force myself to take a break because my stomach won't stop growling, and I need to eat. Instead of scheduling an Uber and going out, I decide to shower, then sneak over to Ethan's and raid his fridge. Surprisingly enough, I don't feel a bit guilty about it.

CHAPTER TWELVE

ETHAN

AFTER HOLDING a meeting with the interns at the studio and setting up for the live preview event I'm hosting this weekend, I decide to call it a day and head home. Admittedly, I'm anxious to see Vada again.

As soon as I walk in, I smell something coming from the kitchen. Once I walk down the hallway and round the corner, I hear sizzling food. Vada's working around the kitchen, completely lost in her own world only wearing a tight tank top and skimpy shorts. Not making her aware of my presence, I lean against the door and cross my arms as I watch her shuffling carefree in front of the stove. I can't help but think how different things might be between us if she didn't live hundreds of miles away and if I didn't have a closet of baggage.

She turns around and gasps when she sees I've been watching her.

"Jesus!" She presses a hand to her chest as she breathes heavily.

"I'm sorry," I say with a smile. "Not too often is there a beautiful woman in my kitchen cooking *me* dinner."

Vada places a hand on her hip with a spatula between her fingers. "I wasn't cooking dinner for you." Her cute laugh gives her away.

Crossing the room, I peek in the skillet and see several hamburger patties. "So you're going to eat a quadruple burger?" I raise my brows, knowing she's full of shit. "I'd actually like to watch that. Love a woman with an *appetite*."

She laughs. "Yeah, a *sexual* appetite."

"Obviously. Because I'm an all-you-can-eat buffet, babe." I look her up and down, taking my time on her curves and breasts before meeting her eyes. A smile touches her lips, and her eyebrow pops up.

"Really? How much does that cost?" She chuckles.

"Just one night." I'm tempted to lean her against the counter and devour her for dinner, but considering the macaroni is about to boil over, I wait. After turning off the burner, she finishes up and carefully places the food on two plates.

Before sitting down, I grab her cheeks in my palms, lean in and brush my lips against hers. Closing my eyes, I focus on her mouth as I run my fingers through her hair noticing how much she smells like vanilla and coffee. Vada melts against my touch, and for a moment I'm lost in the sweet taste of her. Grabbing her bottom lip between my teeth, I tug and suck on it before barely inching away from her mouth. I steady her as she looks at my lips with hooded eyes.

"Sorry, I've been thinking about doing that all damn day."

"All right, Casanova. Let's eat," she whispers. "Before it gets cold, please."

"Only because you asked nicely. Maybe you'll end up learning some manners after all. I have to warn ya though, those damn yankees aren't used to it." I tease with a wink as I add mayonnaise to my bread.

We eat while making small talk, and I realize how much I need to have her, taste her again. I'm a greedy bastard, but our time is limited.

The hamburger basically melts in my mouth. I can't remember the last time someone, other than my mom or Aunt Millie, cooked for me. It's a nice surprise.

"Dinner is delicious, by the way. Who knew writers were decent in the kitchen, too?"

"We are a species of many talents," she gloats.

"Well, I appreciate it. Sure beats the PB&J sandwich I was going to make."

She flashes me a genuine smile while taking the smallest bite of macaroni and cheese.

"So did you get a lot written today?" I ask, honestly curious.

"Actually." She clears her throat and smiles. "I did."

"Well, that's why you came here, right?"

"Yeah, it must be the country livin' or something," she says without cracking a smile, although we both know the inside joke to that.

She grins, and I can't deny how excited I get when I see her smile.

"Glad to hear it." I smirk. "Mac 'n cheese, good choice."

"I would've cooked veggies or something healthy as a side, but you've got macaroni and cheese for days, probably months," she says, changing the subject.

"My mama likes to make sure I'm eating. Between her and Aunt Millie, I've got enough to feed a football team."

"Or an army," she adds, which causes me to chuckle. There were several dinners missed as I worked until the sun came up. I completely engulfed myself with learning and becoming better at my craft. Work became nonstop, which is why Aunt Millie continues to randomly bring me food. She was never able to have kids of her own, so she's always treated me like a son.

My mama and her both knew I was wasting away in this house. After I lost everything that ever meant a damn to me, what was I supposed to do? This was the home Alana and I shared and the last place we were together.

Though the smell of her has faded with the years, sometimes when I'm trying to fall asleep, I can hear her voice asking if everything is okay. Losing Alana broke me into a million different pieces that can never be put back together. Though years have passed, I'll never be the man I used to be. Life didn't prepare me for the day I lost my best friend, wife, and lover. Nothing could have. Where love once lived, there's nothing but emptiness. That old saying, *It's better to have loved and lost than to not have loved at all,* is total bullshit.

I'm lost in my thoughts, but Vada somehow pulls me from my mind fuck memories.

"Maybe you should give those who rent the cottage a box of mac 'n cheese as a rental warming gift?" She laughs.

"Might need to send them all home with you, because I wouldn't be surprised if you sit at your computer eating a jar of Nutella with your finger when you have a book due," I say, trying to finish my burger, recalling her bad eating habits when she's on deadline.

"Ha! That's pretty accurate actually. One time I finished an entire jar of peanut butter in a week. Kept it by my laptop, and each time I took a break, I'd eat a few spoonfuls."

"I didn't realize you loved nuts so much. Should've though." I chuckle, which earns me a playful, much deserved eyeroll.

After we're finished with dinner, Vada places our plates in the sink. As I stand, she looks at me over her shoulder with a smile as if she knows I'm about to claim her as mine for the night.

"I really have to finish this one chapter." She interrupts the dirty thoughts streaming through my head.

I run my tongue along my lower lip, and her eyes follow. She's officially under my trance. "How long do you need?"

As she glances down at my hardness, I adjust myself. My dick wants more of what it had last night, and I'm not protesting. In fact, I'm fucking dying to be back inside her.

"An hour," she says. "Then I think I'll need a refill of inspiration."

"You mean more of my cock?" I cross my arms over my chest and laugh when she squirms.

"Are you always so direct?" she asks, turning her body around to face me.

"What do you think?" I inch closer to her, my breath

crawling over her skin, which causes her to shiver. Her mouth falls open when she feels my length against her leg.

"I can see the anaconda is back. Should probably get going before I get a snake bite." She chuckles.

"Oh, Vada," I drawl. "You've already been bitten, and there's no antivenom that can save you from me now." I hum against her ear, lightly brushing my fingers across the bare skin on her stomach.

"Holy shit…" she whispers, her eyes fluttering closed, and I can feel her melt against me.

I lean in, pinching the skin of her neck between my teeth then trace the shell of her ear with my mouth. "Go write your chapter." I glance at my phone, then set a timer. "One hour."

I know by the flush color of her cheeks and how her nipples stand at full attention, that she's forcing herself to go write, which makes me smile. She may only be here for a few more days, but I'm going to try to make the most of it. I'll give her an hour, but just one, then she'll get exactly what she wants and needs to finish that damn book.

Once Vada rushes to the cottage, Wilma pounces down the stairs, and I place some wet food in her bowl. She stretches as if she's playing hard to get with her food.

"Stop showing off," I tell her and receive a sweet meow in response. Bending over, I pet her before she walks to her bowl because she can't be bothered when she's eating. I climb the stairs two at a time and head for the shower because I'm sweaty from working so hard at the studio today. As soon as the warm water hits my body, I allow myself to relax. I under-stand what Vada means when she talks about being wound up real tight. We're more alike than she knows.

As I wash over my muscles, I think back to the conversation I had with Millie this morning.

"Didn't think you allowed women to stay the night. It was one of your unspoken bachelor rules or something." She pushed for confirmation as she pulled eggs and bacon from the fridge.

"Aunt Millie, please," I begged, pulling a coffee cup out of the cabinet. It was weird talking about my sex life with my aunt, but she always liked to pry and keep up with me considering I haven't settled down after Alana. Don't plan on committing to anyone either and that drives her insane.

"You know why I'm here, hon. I wanted to make sure you're doing okay." She looked at me with concern written on her face.

"I'm fine, seriously." Though I'm not, and she could see right through it.

I place my hand against the shower wall and stand there until the water runs cold, which forces me to get out and dry off. So much can happen in a short amount of time, and when my life was turned upside down, then completely destroyed, I realized that. Most people say time makes it easier, but that couldn't be more wrong. Usually, I try to stay busy, keep my head down, my heart guarded, and my mind somewhere else. This is why I planned a big live demo for this specific weekend at the studio because being around people helps keep my thoughts away from the darkness that tends to haunt me. Another reason why Vada is a Godsend. She's the perfect distraction and might be the only thing keeping me from self-destructing.

I try to push the thoughts out of my head and think of

something else because my mood is turning sour quickly. Looking down at my phone, I notice I have thirty minutes before I can forget everything that's swirling through my head and focus purely on Vada. *And in Vada.*

After I'm dressed, I make the climb up the stairs to the tower. The warm glow from the lights reflect below, and from a distance, I'm sure the tower shines like a beacon in the darkness. I try to clean up a bit, but I can't seem to focus. The kiln is full of mugs I made earlier in the week and won't be ready for another twenty-four hours. However, as I look around the room, I can't help but feel a tug at my heart. So much has changed, but some things are exactly the same—this room being one of them.

Before I get too caught up, my phone vibrates in my pocket, and I know time's up. I turn it off, climb down both sets of stairs, and walk through the back door. As I cross the garden, I see Vada sitting at the desk in front of the window of the cottage. Her fingers are flying against the keys, and she barely stops. Chuckling, I wait until I see her fingers come to a halt. While she reads over what she wrote, her lips move, and when she finishes, she sits back and smiles. The look on her face is pure satisfaction. At this very moment, Vada is so happy, that it's contagious.

Taking this as my cue, I walk down the path leading to the cottage. Sucking in a deep breath, I knock three times on the door. I hear Vada rushing around inside, and when the door swings open, I give her a knowing smile.

"It's already been an hour?" she asks. The look on her face tells me she lost track of time.

I don't give her an answer but take a few steps forward,

until our lips collide, causing waves of want to rush through me. Vada sighs against my mouth before coming in for more as I kick the door shut with my foot. Taking no time at all, she begins unbuttoning my pants, then unzipping them.

"I want you so fucking bad." She moans as she forces my shirt above my head.

"I'm supposed to be undressing you," I tell her, doing exactly that.

Within moments, our clothes are on the floor, and she's standing in front of me naked. Taking my time, I memorize her body with my hands and lips. Her head falls back on her shoulders as I place a perky nipple in my mouth. Kissing across her chest, I make sure to give the other the same attention. Threading her fingers through my hair, Vada lets out a greedy moan which only causes me to smile. She's ravenous, and I love it, especially when she pushes me down on the bed, like a savage, taking exactly what she wants. I pull the condom out of my pocket, and she takes it from my hand and rolls it down my shaft, then slides on top of me.

"Oh my fuck," I say, as she throws her head back, and rides me hard and long.

"Yes, yes," she mutters, taking full control. Her breasts bounce with each time she rocks from the tip down to the bottom of my shaft. Taking some sort of control back, I thumb her clit, which only drives her wilder.

I like this side of Vada, the woman who takes control and takes exactly what she wants.

She leans over, brushing her lips against mine. "Ethan, I'm about to come."

"Do it, babe. I love watching you."

Tossing her head back, her mouth falls open, and she rides me slow, rocking her hips in circles.

"Yes, don't stop," she begs sucking in air, enjoying every second as I circle her clit.

"Never," I whisper, secretly wishing this week wouldn't end as I watch her lose herself on top of me.

CHAPTER THIRTEEN

VADA

I FIND myself chasing the white rabbit, as curious as the young Alice from *Alice in Wonderland*, only to be transported to a world other than my own. I'm falling down a never-ending rabbit hole as Ethan forces me to forget all the beliefs I had about casual sex.

He has me second-guessing everything and doesn't even know it.

My eyes flutter open, and I watch him, watching me ride him. As I scratch my nails down his chest and let out moans loud enough the whole neighborhood can hear, I realize I've actually become the sex-crazed woman in my book. My body is fully his, in every sense, and with each thrust, I crumble to dust with him. The orgasm rocks and shakes me so greatly that it can't be measured on the Richter scale.

As I float back to reality, I topple on top of him. Ethan's lips trace mine, and I know by the soft look on his face, that he'll unravel at any moment. His heavy breaths in my ear combined with long, deep movements have my body screaming out in protest, but the problem is I want more of him, *all* of him. Knowing this will all end when I leave for Chicago, I try to memorize every inch of him. With my legs wrapped tightly around his hips, he grabs my ass and lifts me slightly, controlling every deep thrust, giving me everything he is.

"Harder," I whisper sinking on him, wanting him to rip me in two, so half of me can stay here while the other half returns home.

Without hesitation, he does exactly that.

"Fuck," Ethan pants. "Vada," he says one last time before his body seizes and finally relaxes. We briefly stay like that, the closest two human beings can possibly be, and oddly enough, it's comforting. Ethan gives me a long, needy kiss before pulling away.

Once we've cleaned up and caught our breaths, he crawls into bed and pulls me into his arms. The moment is so intimate that my heart does a quick flutter, which slightly confuses me. *Why am I feeling like this is becoming more than just sex?* I wrap my arm around his waist as his fingers draw circles on my bare skin. I try really hard to push the thoughts away, but it's like my mind wants to convince me that this feels different. It feels right. But it can't. As I rest my head on his chest with his arms wrapped tight around me, I'm fighting an internal battle that I'm not sure I'll win.

It's just sex. I try repeating it over and over, but my heart betrays me.

Swallowing hard, I look up into his honey-colored eyes, and smile. "I could get used to this, E," I admit, honestly, putting my heart out on the line.

As soon as the words leave my mouth, I regret them immediately. Ethan tenses and forces a smile, but I notice he's uneasy. His eyes narrow, saying so much, but hiding secrets. I can't tell if it's anger or sadness or a combination of the both, and it confuses me. I want to pry and ask questions, but instead, I offer an apology. Saying anything at all was stupid, especially when he's made it very clear that this is temporary and that he doesn't do relationships. Honestly, I don't know what I expected.

"I'm sorry," I whisper. "That came out wrong," is all I offer as an explanation. His heartbeat vibrates hard in his chest, and I feel like an idiot for saying those words aloud.

"Goodnight, Vada," he whispers, leaning over and turning off the lamp next to the bed, then pulling me back into position. Ethan holds me tight as if he doesn't want to let me go. I fall asleep in his arms, listening to the rhythmic beat of his heart.

I roll over and reach for Ethan, only to wake up to an empty, cold bed. There's nothing but crumpled sheets and a blanket where his body was just hours ago. Still half-asleep, I sit up and look around the room, hoping to see him here still. My clothes are exactly where I left them last night, but Ethan's aren't. I didn't realize waking up alone after a night like that would leave me feeling so empty. Instantly, my mind goes to a negative place, but I try not to allow my insecurities to get the best of me.

After I stretch, I head for the shower hoping it will relax my muscles and mind. It feels as if I did gymnastics all night, but I guess in a roundabout way I did. My body is definitely not used to this.

The water somewhat calms me and does exactly what I want, but I can't help but think about my past and all the bad relationships I've experienced over the years. Trying as hard as I can, I push those thoughts away while I dry off and get dressed.

Once I feel somewhat normal again, I work up the courage to head over to Ethan's just to make sure everything is okay. I mean, I know this is purely physical, and I shouldn't be concerned, but I am. Last night as we were falling asleep after I said what I was thinking, he immediately tensed up. It wasn't the first time my honesty has ruined a good moment and knowing me, I'm sure it won't be the last.

As I walk down the path that leads to his house, I see Henry coming at me at a full sprint.

"Shit. Go away, Henry!" I scream and run toward the back door, somehow making it in before he can attack me.

I look out the window of the back door, and he's standing there, looking straight into my eyes.

"You're an asshole," I say to him as he pecks around, agitating me.

I suck in a deep breath, turn around, and listen. The house is quiet, but coffee has been brewed, and there's dishes in the sink. I close my eyes tight and open them before I decide to make my way up the stairs. For some reason, my heart is pounding hard in my chest. My adrenaline spikes as I reach the second floor.

"Ethan?" I whisper and wait. I don't hear anything, so I walk to his room and open the door. The bed is perfectly made, so I doubt he came back and went to sleep. Just as I'm turning to walk up the second set of stairs that lead to the tower, I notice the door I've never gone through is partially open. I've been in the bathroom, guestroom, and bedroom, so this room has me intrigued. Knowing I should walk past it and respect his privacy, curiosity gets the best of me. Instead, I stop, place my fingers around the wooden door and slightly push it open until I can peek inside.

My mouth goes dry when I see a light pink painted room with a dark wooden baby crib on one side. The walls are decorated with pictures and vinyl cut-outs of Eiffel Towers, and when I look at the wall above the crib, I notice wooden-painted letters spelling the word, *Paris*. A rocking chair sits in the corner facing the big bay window with a cute nightstand next to it. There's a changing table and dresser on the other side. It's obvious this is a nursery and a gorgeous one at that, but confusion ripples through me because I know Ethan doesn't have a child.

"What the fuck are you doing?" an angry voice growls from behind and startles me.

I still and turn my body toward him. He moves around me, grabs the doorknob and slams the door shut.

"I'm sorry, I…" I begin, but I have no words to explain the reason why I opened that door other than being curious and wanting to know more about the man I'm sleeping with, but I know that's not a good enough reason. Seeing him look at me now, I feel like complete shit for invading his privacy and exposing a secret he's obviously been keeping.

"I think it's time for you to go back to the cottage, Vada." Ethan's voice is monotonous and firm, which pierces straight through my heart. The man standing in front of me isn't the same man I've come to know. The look in his eyes says everything his words don't. He's pissed. I try to reach out to him, but instead, he turns and walks to the stairs that lead to the tower without giving me a second glance.

Minutes pass, and I stand there completely shocked and upset. I want to tell him how sorry I am, but I've learned to give people their space and calm down, though it's not always an easy thing to do. Like a dog with its tail tucked between its legs, I walk down the stairs, through the back door, and across the path until I'm standing inside the cottage.

Emotions swirl through me, and I wish he weren't so upset.

I sit on the edge of the bed and thoughts from my past come rushing in full force.

The rain poured down in buckets as I walked the few blocks home from school. I'd taken a half day and skipped my afternoon classes to surprise my boyfriend for our one-year anniversary. Lucas and I had been living together for a few months, but I knew deep in my heart that at any moment he'd propose, and as soon as I graduated college, we'd get married and start the rest of our lives together. With a bag of Chinese food gripped in my hand and an umbrella in the other, I crossed the street and followed the sidewalk that led up to our apartment building. Once inside, I climbed the flights of stairs and walked down the hall with a cheesy grin on my face.

When I slid the key in the door, I thought I heard a woman's voice, but chalked it up to being exhausted. Once I opened the door, I noticed panties, a bra, a T-shirt, and blue jeans in a line on the floor. The Chinese food slipped from my grasp and slammed to the floor causing a mess. Moans echoed from our bedroom, and my first reaction was to leave, to pretend it wasn't happening because this had to be one big nightmare, but then the anger set in.

I walked down the hall until I was standing in the doorway watching my boyfriend fuck my best friend.

"Are you kidding me?" I screamed out. Horror and anger on my face.

Lucas pushed Emma from on top of him as she tried to hurry and hide her body. Guilt and shame covered them both.

"Get the fuck out," I said in an oddly calm voice. "Both of you, get out right now. I can't stand looking at either of you." I stood my ground, not allowing my emotions to take hold though I felt like I was dying inside. The two people I loved the most betrayed me in the bed I've slept in since I was a kid.

I watched Emma as she wrapped the sheet around her body, not making eye contact as she walked past me and picked up her clothes from the floor.

"Vada, baby. It's not what you think. Emma means nothing to me. I love you," Lucas begged with his dick in his hand—literally.

"So did Emma just fall on your dick or what? Because I'm a little confused as to why you're fucking my best friend in our bed after every-thing I've done for you while you go to law school. You make me sick!" I hissed at him, years of trust issues coming full circle.

He walked over to me, pleading, telling me how much of a mistake it was, but I couldn't listen to his lies anymore. I turned around and walked away. After he realized I wasn't taking his bullshit, he packed a bag of clothes and left. I watched as the two of them walked in the rain together toward her car that was parked a few blocks away. I should've realized everything wasn't perfect like I had built in my head. Our relationship was based on lies and broken promises, and I *was the stupid girl who believed it was going to be my happily ever after.*

After that day, I promised myself I'd never let that happen to me again.

Lucas was smart, but also one of those bad boy types. He lured me in with his charm and hot body. He was also a big flirt, so I shouldn't have been surprised, but in my mind, I created this faux hope that he was different.

I've always been attracted to the wrong guys, even though deep down, I knew they meant trouble and heartbreak. I'm sure Dr. Phil would have a field day psychoanalyzing my attraction to men who are most likely to cheat, lie, and break my heart. After watching the way my father lied and manipulated my mother, it's somehow the only thing I know. What would Freud say? Daddy issues, no doubt.

Lucas, Jason, Brett, Tyler, and Todd. Hell, my ex list is as long as Taylor Swift's.

Lucas was a cheater. *Bastard.*

Jason was a liar and thief. *Money from my wallet just miraculously vanished every time he was around.*

Brett was an alcoholic. *Jack Daniels was a better match for him anyway.*

Tyler was a womanizer. *Apparently charming and sexy are my weaknesses.*

Todd, well, he was gay. *At least he made a great shopping partner.*

I could probably write the lyrics to a breakup song with my track record.

I'll be the first to admit I have trust issues, but how could I not? From as far back as I could remember, he'd verbally abused my mother, and worse, she just took it. He'd drink and lie about it. I swore to myself, that no matter what if a man or anyone ever spoke to me or treated me the way he did her, I would stand up for myself.

And better — I'd fucking walk away.

That didn't leave a lot of room for a meaningful relationship to form.

Many nights I buried myself in books hoping I wouldn't hear him screaming. Reading saved my life. It helped transport me into a world that didn't include my father berating my mother. In books, I found adventure and love and kindness, everything I was missing in my everyday life. Ultimately, reading later inspired me to become a writer and create worlds far better than my own.

As an adult, words became my escape as well, but in a different way. Though the world may be filled with loveless assholes and men who can't give me a happy ending, at least in my books there's always love and happily ever afters.

I stand up, realizing I'm hungry but too embarrassed to go back over to Ethan's. Going to my suitcase, I dig for the extra protein bars I packed for this trip. Once I find one, I go to my laptop and turn it on. I'm in a bad mood. Inspiration has left, but I put my fingers on the keys anyway because these words aren't going to write themselves. I go up one paragraph and read what I wrote before Ethan barged in and stole my breath away.

He looks at her across the small room and moves to her in one quick motion.

"I love you," he whispers across the shell of her ear, causing her to shiver.

Smiling, she bites her bottom lip and whispers the words back to him. How could two star-crossed lovers find their way back to one another so easily? Knowing this might be her last chance to spill her heart before leaving, she goes to him, and presses her lips so softly against his and steals the words that were teetering on his tongue.

Is it possible to be jealous of fictional characters? I'm half-tempted to delete what I've written in this chapter and tear the two lovers apart, only to leave the reader as heartbroken and confused as I am. However, instead of doing something rash, I pick up my phone and schedule an Uber.

When I walk out of the cottage, I look up at the tower and see Ethan staring out the window on the other side. I'm glad his back is to me because I don't think I could look him in the eye without feeling some sort of guilt or awkwardness.

He never mentioned having a daughter, so a nursery was the last thing I expected to see when I opened the door. Having a child means he got someone pregnant and knowing his record, it could've been from a one-night stand, or maybe it was from an actual long-term relationship. If it's with an ex he loved, and they had a child together, maybe that relationship is strained, so he doesn't have custody? Or maybe he only sees his daughter every other week? Different scenarios play in my head, wondering how he could've never mentioned it to me. I know it's not as if he lied to me because we weren't supposed to get personal, but I crossed the line the moment I opened the door that led to his daughter's room. If I could take it back, I would. The look on his face is one I won't forget. His furrowed brows, his intense stare, and his cold tone. He was furious, and everything about his stance and words told me he couldn't trust me. That hurts the most.

Ethan's a broken soul, and while I want to dig deeper, I can't help but feel like I've worn out my welcome.

Dread washes over me as his body turns, and I rush through the garden and hop inside the car that's waiting by the curb.

I don't know where I'm going, but I need to get away and clear my mind.

The countdown until I leave for Chicago begins now.

CHAPTER FOURTEEN

ETHAN

SHE CALLED ME *E,* and it nearly destroyed me. I was seconds away from crumbling.

It's been too long since I heard the nickname Alana used. Considering the anniversary of her death is upon me, waiting to destroy me from the inside out, it was too much to hear coming from Vada's voice.

As soon as I tensed and turned to flick the lights off, I knew she could tell something was bothering me. She assumed it was what she said about getting used to this—us being together— hell, she even apologized for saying it, but I was too lost in my own head to speak.

She didn't know that being called E was the nickname my late wife had for me; she couldn't have, considering I haven't divulged that part of my life to her. It was nothing more than a coincidence, and I wish I could go back and tell her my reaction had nothing to do with her and everything to do with my past, but I was caught off guard.

After Vada falls asleep in my arms, I slide out of bed, put on my clothes, and quietly leave. For hours, I sit in the tower and replay my life and all the events that led me to this very moment. I sit long enough to watch the sun barely peek over the horizon. Pink and purple hues paint across the sky in long painters' wisps, and I feel like I'm smothering in my thoughts to the point where I need some fresh air.

Putting on my shoes, I grab the keys to my car because driving sometimes helps clear my mind. I head down familiar streets, but nothing looks the same. Though I have nowhere to go, I follow pavement until I'm driving under the Magnolia Cemetery archway. As soon as I pull in, a heavy weight presses on my chest.

Every year on this day I visit, even though it brings me back to all those memories and makes me miss them even more. It was hard to come here at first, especially that first year, but after a few times, it became a little easier. Though being here will never be considered easy.

Sucking in a deep breath, I park at the edge of the street and walk across the plush grass to the oak trees by the river. As soon as I see the black marble of Alana's headstone, I almost fall to my knees.

No matter how much time passes, seeing their names engraved in stone always brings me back to the moment in the hospital when I found out Alana was gone. The only sliver of happiness I felt was knowing I had a piece of Alana in Paris until my sweet baby girl passed away soon after.

The pain in my heart is almost too much to bear as I read their names, *Alana and Paris Rochester* together. Burying my wife and child made me second guess everything about life, espe-cially the *whys*.

"My girls," I whisper softly, tracing their names with my finger on the cool stone. It was never supposed to be like this. We were supposed to have a handful of kids and grow old and happy together in our house on the small hill by the creek. I was supposed to watch my daughter take her first steps, hear her say her first words, watch her play at the playground, and go to her first day of kindergarten.

So many things that were taken from me.

I'll forever be robbed of those memories and of ones I'll never be able to experience. Her walking across the stage to graduate high school, driving her to college, and eventually walking her down the aisle.

Covering my face with my hands, I try to get a hold of myself, but it's a losing battle. The *should-have-beens* are enough to drive me crazy.

Sitting here under the oak tree is the only time I allow myself to fully give in to what happened. At the funerals, I was in a perpetual state of shock. Hell, for the last five years I have been. Most of the time, I try to keep my pain and loss buried deep. But being here, like this, there's no escaping my reality. I'd give anything to be able to hold the two of them again.

The cool morning breeze brushes over my skin, and I wish it could take all the pain away, but it never does. When I'm here, it's as if time stands completely still.

"Aunt Millie says you'd want me to be happy." I wait as if I'm going to hear her voice speak back to me. Nothing but the wind rustling the leaves on the trees can be heard.

"I know deep in my heart you'd want me to be happy and continue living my life, but I don't know if I can. Every day, I think about you. I think about Paris. I think about what we could have had. Where the three of us would be right now at this very moment. The studio is everything you wished it would be. It's doing so well, and I know you'd be proud."

A single tear streams down my face and splashes on my hand. I didn't even realize I was crying. I tell myself that out here, it's okay to feel something. It's okay to let those emotions take ahold of me. I close my eyes and find what I'm trying to say.

"I met someone." I let out a stifled laugh. "And you'd love her. She doesn't take my shit or let me say whatever I want. Aunt Millie met her too and basically gave her approval, but you know how she is—she likes anyone who isn't afraid to call me out on my shit."

Many times, Aunt Millie and Alana would gang up against me, and I find myself smiling about it now. I know it's been five long years of trying to find a way to cope and heal the shattered pieces of my heart, but this is the first time I've ever spoken those words. Moving on—I've been against it. However, being here today, knowing Vada is back at the cottage waiting for me, feels different this time.

"I'll always love you and our baby, Alana." But I know she knew that. No matter what happens in my life, Alana and Paris will hold a special place in my heart—always and forever. Trying to pick up the pieces and move on doesn't mean I'll forget them. I have to remind myself this even though Mama has told me that a million times.

"I don't know what to do," I say, wishing she were here. "I

just…I wish you could tell me that it was okay, that you'd want me to move on so I'd stop feeling guilty at the thought of it." I sit and wait, but not surprisingly, nothing miraculous happens. After a while, the sun beams down on my skin, and I know it's time to go. I look at the grave one more time before I walk back to my car.

By the time I make it home, I'm emotionally and physically exhausted. I sit on the couch and fall asleep thinking of her.

Alana walks through the kitchen with a smile on her face, leaning against the doorway. I rub my eyes, not believing what I'm seeing.

"I know I'm dreaming," I say.

Walking across the room, she sits next to me. I glance down and see the wedding ring on her finger, and somehow mine is there, too. Though I wore it for years after her death, I stopped wearing it when I almost lost it while working on a piece. I wanted to keep it close to me still, so I keep it in the drawer of my nightstand along with Paris' footprints.

She grabs my hand and gives me a wink. "Ethan," she says, in that tone I was so used to hearing.

I look into her blue eyes, pulling her into my arms, never wanting to wake, never wanting to let go.

She leans back, pulling us apart. "Vada seems like she's perfect for you. So what the hell are you waiting for, E? You have to live your life. You have to learn to be happy again, and you deserve to be."

"But…" I try to protest.

She places her finger on my lips and stops my words though I have so much to say. "You have to take a leap of faith."

I wake, my heart pounding rapidly in my chest. Sweat covers my brow, and I thought I heard her voice, here in the room with me. My throat is dry, and I replay the conversation so many times I feel like I'm losing my mind. I asked for a sign, or maybe my subconscious is playing tricks on me, but there it was, and it felt so real. This isn't the first time Alana has visited me in my dreams, but it's never been so vivid.

Needing a shower, I climb the stairs. As I round the corner, I'm shocked to see Vada in the hallway, staring into Paris' room. At first, I don't know what to say or do, so I stand there stunned. I'm not ready to talk about it just yet, not when I'm in this fragile state of mind.

As soon as the words fly out of my mouth and she turns around, it's obvious I took her by surprise. I slam the door shut and she immediately begins to apologize, but I shut her out and go to the tower. Closing myself tight doesn't solve anything, but I need this time to think. I need to find my words and tell her the truth, as hard as that's going to be, but I feel like she deserves to know. The only problem is, where do I even start?

Most people in the area know my backstory and how I was a widower before I turned twenty-five. Most of the women I bring home don't mention it or even allude they know. I was the talk of the town for a while, especially after Paris Pottery & Studio opened. It was my way of honoring my baby girl and wife. It was how I kept and continue to keep their spirit alive. People loved Alana's pottery, and before her belly got too big, she was quickly becoming a hometown sensation. Between Millie and Mama peddling Alana's mugs out of their trunks after church, the news of her work traveled quickly, but not as fast as her death. It rocked everyone who knew her.

It destroyed me.

After I have time to myself, I realize I acted like a complete asshole to Vada and guilt washes over me. Not that it's an excuse, but visiting the cemetery left my wounds freshly cut open, but that's not her fault. She has no idea how broken I've been over the years, and how she may be the glue that can put me back together. I feel that deep in my heart, so strongly, that it almost knocks me down. Vada came barreling into my life with that smart mouth and sass, and soon she'll be leaving to go back to Chicago. Time is running out, and like a dream, she'll be gone, too.

Just as I'm about to head to the cottage and apologize, I see Vada leave in a rush, and it wears on me. I don't want to seem crazy and call her since I have her number from the booking, so I wait. This is something that needs to be discussed in person anyway.

While she's gone, I take a shower and try to get some much-needed sleep. Once I'm rested, I brew some coffee then go back up into the tower, turn on some music, and busy myself in my work for hours.

Before dark, I hear a car door slam, and from the tower I see Vada walk across the sidewalk with a Starbucks cup in one hand and shopping bags in the other. I watch her go straight to the cottage, shut the door, and close the curtains. Feeling nervous, I wash the extra clay from my hands and find an ounce of courage as I go to her. Once I'm at the cottage door, I knock, but she doesn't answer.

"Okay then," I say, turning around and heading back to the house.

"Ethan?" I immediately turn around and notice a towel wrapped tightly around her body, accentuating her curves. The late summer breeze carries the smell of her strawberry soap, which causes me to smile.

I walk toward her, but she stands in the doorway with her arms holding the towel. Water drips from the tips of her hair, and she smells so damn good. Vada looks me up and down, noticing the clay on my pants and shirt, and she almost takes a step back.

"I've got a lot of explainin' to do," I tell her, hoping she'll hear me out.

"You don't owe me anything, Casanova. I was the one who violated your space," she says, timidly, and I hate I've made her feel that way.

"Well, I *do* owe you an apology. I'm sorry, Vada. I hope you forgive me for being a total and utter asshole today. There's a lot on my mind, but that's no excuse for how I treated you. You don't deserve that—ever," I reassure her because it's the truth.

Her shoulders relax, and she slightly smiles. "Apology accepted."

"Do you have plans tomorrow night?" I slyly ask.

She looks at me like I've lost my mind. "Other than trying to write a book, my schedule's wide open."

"I'd be obliged if you'd accompany me on a date tomorrow night around seven," I say over insinuating my drawl and tipping my imaginary hat in her direction.

Now she's really looking at me like I'm crazy. "Seriously?"

"Yes, ma'am. Serious as eating ribs on the 4th of July."

Her laughter echoes through the garden. "Actually, I think I might need to wash my hair tomorrow night around that time."

I take a few steps closer; our bodies are almost touching. "I'm not the type of man to beg…"

"Bad boys never beg," she says right before our lips softly meet.

As she kisses me, the worry melts away. The anxiety of everything swirling in my head temporarily disappears. In this moment, it's just me and Vada, and I'm thankful she's able to rescue me, even if she has no idea.

CHAPTER FIFTEEN

VADA

"I HAVEN'T BEEN on a real date in years. I don't know what to wear," I tell Nora over the phone because she's my go-to in situations like this. Actually, she's my only person considering I don't have anyone to ask.

"Go sassy with a touch of slutty. Guys love that," she says matter-of-factly.

"Oh my God. How do you know that?" I let out a laugh, emptying my suitcase on the bed. Nora doesn't do dates, and the only time she gets out of the house is to go to the grocery store or visit her best friend. Considering the woman is in her mid-sixties, I imagine her version of slutty and mine are two totally different things.

"I watch a lot of television shows. I'm sure it's the same in real life," she tells me, amused with herself.

I roll my eyes, and I'm glad she can't see me because she'd totally call me out for it. "Okay, well hug Oliver for me, and tell him I'll see him soon. I'll call you in the morning and let you know how it goes," I say, trying to piece clothes together to make some sort of outfit that doesn't look like I'm going to bed or to the gym.

"You already know how I feel about him. And you better call me. You know I'll be up all night worrying about you otherwise."

"I'm sure you will. I promise I'll call." And I will. Nora cares about my life more than my own mother, and I'm happy someone does, even if she pretends to hate Oliver. Usually, my life is monotonous, and I live the same schedule over and over. To have some sort of action has got to be entertaining for her.

We say our goodbyes, and I throw my cell phone on the bed, right next to a sundress I bought on a whim yesterday while I was out. Slipping it on, and seeing how it fits in the full-length mirror, I know I've found a winner. Considering it's late summer in Charleston, the evenings are still warm so this will have to do. Pinning my hair to the side and putting on a hint of makeup, I sit down at my computer and am able to type a few pages before a knock echoes through the cottage, pulling me away.

Instantly, my heart flutters as I cross the room and open the door. Ethan greets me with a sexy smile wearing a blue, button-up shirt and slacks.

"You clean up nicely, Casanova."

Pulling me into his arms, our lips crash together, causing the butterflies inside me to swarm in circles. Taking our time, we kiss until our lips are swollen, until I feel like I can't breathe. There was a moment when I didn't think we'd make it out of the cottage.

"You're beautiful, Vada," he whispers across my lips,

setting the tone of this date. Blush hits my cheeks as soon as Ethan tucks loose hair behind my ear, his fingertips grazing the softness of my neck. Once I close the cottage door, Ethan leads me down the sidewalk.

After seeing him, I feel completely underdressed for the occasion, and my nerves start to get the best of me.

"What?" I ask as he looks over at me with a smirk on his lips. I wait for his answer as we continue walking forward.

"Just thinking about taking that dress off you later," he teases, opening the door to his car for me. "Hope it wasn't expensive." He winks.

His words make me laugh and slightly relax. Once I'm inside the car, I take the moment to suck in a deep breath.

Ethan climbs in and buckles then starts the engine. "Everything okay?"

"Just nervous, I guess," I say honestly, buckling myself in.

"Don't worry. I left my cock at home," he teases, and all the worry I had of the evening melts away just like that.

We drive through town, and I'm confused when Ethan doesn't slow. I turn to him, ready to ask where we're going once we cross the second bridge.

"I thought we'd go somewhere on the outskirts of town that's more intimate, away from all the touristy stuff," he explains when he notices my perplexed expression. "You can do that any day of the week."

"Oh, so I'm getting the exclusive Rochester treatment tonight?"

Ethan chuckles. "Babe, you've been getting that all week."

Soon we're pulling into the parking lot of a restaurant that's decorated with parts from old boats. Oars, anchors, and ropes are hung on the building, and when we step inside, I realize it's the entire theme of the place. I immediately fall in love with it. We're swiftly escorted through the quaint dining area onto the patio. Our table overlooks the white sand and dark blue water, and in the distance, I hear the waves crashing against the shore. Glancing over the candle that lights Ethan's face, I find myself smiling.

"This is perfect," I whisper to him, admiring his messy hair and the smirk on his lips. Though there's a few couples on the patio, it feels like it's only Ethan and me in this moment.

The waitress walks up, and Ethan orders everything down to my favorite wine.

She returns with a bottle of Cabernet and a basket of hot bread.

"How'd you know about the wine?" I ask.

"Google," he jokes.

"Oh, stop. You didn't Google me."

"I did," he admits, shamelessly. "Even ordered a few copies of your books to put on the shelf in the cottage for the other guests who rent it. Might actually update the Airbnb listing and tell them the world-famous Vada Collins wrote her upcoming bestselling novel there. It will be as popular as the Stanley Hotel lobby in Stephen King's *The Shining*."

I actually snort. "I hope that works out for you. Could actually become a little cash cow of sorts. People will drive by and stop to take pictures with the cottage. I'll send you a headshot to hang on the wall." I wink.

Being like this with him feels so easy and natural. It's strange how a person can meet someone, and within a few days, it feels like old friends who've known each other for years.

Soon our food arrives, and I can't wait to dig into the Etoufee Flounder Ethan ordered us both. Apparently, it's a southern favorite, and I actually let out a moan when I take the first bite of fish. The sauce, mashed potatoes, everything is simply delicious.

"Told you," he says, noticing how much I love it.

"I'm never leaving Charleston," I kid as I take another bite.

"I wish you wouldn't," Ethan says, his tone more serious than before.

His words catch me off guard, and I open my mouth then close it, not really knowing what to say. My whole life is back in Chicago, and I know it was inevitable that this week would end. We both knew.

"I love Charleston because it's a little bit of city and a whole lot of southern. But mainly because we have everything here, the history, culinary scene, and more. What's not to love about Charleston?" he asks, quickly changing the subject.

After we're finished eating, he pays, grabs a blanket from the car, then takes my hand and leads me down the wooden path that points to the beach. The sun dips below the horizon and twilight is upon us. The light breeze brushes over my skin, and soon we're touching sand. He bends over and removes his shoes, and I do too.

"I have a lot to tell you, Vada." The light breeze carries his voice.

"Actually, I want to apologize to you, Ethan. I didn't mean to snoop, and I'm really sorry for doing so." I look at him, trying to read his facial expression, hoping he understands.

"Trust is such a big part of my life, and I felt like I broke that with you."

Ethan shakes his head at me. "No, no. You have nothing to apologize about."

We continue walking down the beach, allowing the sand to squish between our toes. Once we're away from the board-walk, Ethan stops and lays the blanket on the ground, then sits. Looking up at me, he pats next to him, and I set my shoes down and join him. Our arms brush together, and goose bumps travel across my skin. I nervously laugh, and Ethan does, too, as he stares out at the rippling waves.

"I was married," he starts, his words catching me off guard. I suspected he had some kind of relationship previously, but I hadn't figured he was divorced.

"But you're not anymore, right?" Suddenly I realize I haven't asked this question. My mind starts playing out all these scenarios of him still being married, which would make me a homewrecker. He doesn't wear a wedding ring, but that doesn't mean anything considering his line of work. As I sit here, I realized how I trusted him so easily, that it makes me almost feel stupid for not making sure beforehand.

Letting out a light laugh, he reassures me by shaking his head. "No, I'm not. She passed away five years ago."

The blood rushes from my face, and the wine from earlier feels like it's finally kicking in.

"I'm so sorry." I try to offer some sort of condolence, but I'm at a loss.

"It was sudden and unexpected." His tone is somber, and I want nothing more than to comfort him. This explains so much about him, and I'm already getting emotional without even knowing the details.

I wait patiently, not wanting to rush him. He continues when he's ready and tells me about Alana and exactly what happened. As I sit next to him on the blanket, tears stream down my face. I can't imagine being so young and losing someone so close.

"So I'm sorry for pushing you away. I've got issues that I'm still working on. But after reacting the way I did, I felt you deserved to know the truth."

"Thank you." I weave my fingers through his. "For trusting me enough to tell me. I'm sure it wasn't easy."

"It's the first time I've told her story to anyone," he admits, my heart swelling. "Southern town, lots of gossips—didn't take long for everyone to hear."

"I appreciate you sharing it with me." I flash a small smile, realizing how big of a step this is for him. "So your daughter?" I swallow hard, not wanting to push my boundaries, but he knows I saw the room that was set up for her.

Ethan sucks in a deep breath as if he's finding the courage to speak.

"Paris came two months early and fought to breathe from the moment she was born. The tubes, the beeping of the machines, sometimes when I'm sitting in a quiet room, I can still hear it all as if I'm there. I think she died of a broken heart though. Once Alana was gone, it seemed Paris' likelihood of surviving diminished greatly. It's like she knew her mama was gone. Ultimately, she was too little, too sick, too weak. She ended up getting meningitis, which came with its own set of complications, and passed away two weeks later."

Ethan swallows down tears, and I see him fighting his emotions, which completely ruins me from the inside out. There's something about watching a man be so vulnerable that breaks me down. I'm so upset over this, and I'm crying for him and everything he's lost. His life was flipped upside down in a matter of weeks.

Regardless, he continues. "The first time I held her was when they unhooked her small body from the machines after she was gone." He covers his face with his hands.

I place my hand on his back, and he falls into my arms. Ethan holds me as if he's falling, and I don't let go. I can't let go, not when I feel like he's breaking in my arms. The pain he feels streams through me, and I wish I could take it all away.

"I don't believe everything happens for a reason. It's a bullshit thing that doesn't bring comfort to anyone. No one should ever have to endure such loss—ever. I'm so sorry, Ethan. I'm sorry this happened to you. And I'm sorry you're having to talk to me about it."

He sits up and rubs his palms over his eyes. With a helpless shrug, he reiterates, "You deserved to know, Vada. Maybe I'm actually losing my mind, but…" He swallows hard. "You're not like everyone else. Being with you is different. I feel like when I'm with you, I can be myself again, and that's a feeling I haven't felt for a very, very long time."

I suck in air, and it almost hits me like a pound of bricks when the realization sets in that he's right. It *has* been different being with him.

"I know what you mean," I admit with a smile on my face, staring into his honey-colored eyes. For a moment, no words exchange between us but so much is being said. My heartbeat rushes, and I wonder if he can feel it, too. Ethan Rochester is more than what I ever bargained for, and after tonight, I see him in a completely different light. I truly understand him on a deeper level—something I haven't ever felt with anyone else.

Ethan leans back on the blanket and pulls me down with him. The light breeze drifts over our bodies as he holds me in his arms. We look up at the stars twinkling in the sky, and in this moment, I don't want to be anywhere else in the world. Our hearts, our bodies, everything is perfectly in sync, and the thought almost frightens me.

"Thank you," Ethan whispers after minutes of silence between us.

I sit up on my elbow and look at him, the moonlight casting a shadow on his beautiful features. "For what?"

"For listening, for allowing me to be myself. For not looking at me like I've grown a second head or anything."

I give him a sweet smile, and he pulls me close. His hot breath kisses my skin, and it's almost too much for me to handle. "You had me at hello, you know that?"

I wasn't expecting to hear that come from his lips. "Ethan—"

"Don't." He stops me, sitting up and pulling me to his chest. My mouth hovers above his until he slightly leans up and claims my lips as his, completely stealing my breath and heart in the flicker of a moment. His kiss is so raw that it almost reaches bone as he cuts me open with the emotion that's streaming from this kiss. The shift I feel is so powerful, it's almost as if the entire world tilts on its axis.

CHAPTER SIXTEEN

ETHAN

I wish I could capture Vada so she'd stay with me here in this moment—as the waves crash in the distance—forever. Right now, I don't feel sadness or pain. I only feel that strange sensation that what we have is bigger than either of us realize. I'm not one to fall for anyone so quickly. Hell, if anything, I've pushed plenty of opportunities away, but with Vada, it's different. She's got me under her spell, and I doubt she's going to let me go before she heads back to Chicago in a couple days. The realization of that completely rips through me, but I keep it to myself.

We lay on the blanket for a while, until I feel Vada shiver.

"Come on, let's go," I tell her, sitting up. "The night's still young. What do you want to do?"

Vada looks at me seductively, and I'm almost tempted to throw her over my shoulder and carry her back to the car because it would be faster.

"Say no more." Standing up, I grab my shoes and slip them

back on. She follows my lead and tries to help me pop sand out of the blanket.

On the drive back to the house, I interlock Vada's fingers with mine. It's a simple, but intimate gesture. I haven't felt the need to hold hands with a woman in years, and now I don't want to let hers go.

"I've got a surprise for you," I say, unbuckling. She follows suit and meets me in front of the car.

Grabbing for her hand again, we walk up the steps to the house where I lead her up the stairs to my bathroom. I light candles and place them around the white iron claw-foot tub. Turning on the hot water until it's steaming, I take my time undressing her, kissing her collarbone and along her shoulder. Her head falls to one side, and she lets out a long sigh as my fingers sweep across the soft skin of her stomach. As I undo each button of my shirt, she watches me intently, not speaking a word.

"How would you write a scene like this?" I ask her, wanting to know the eloquent words she'd use.

She shakes her head. "You don't even want to know."

"I do; come on. I know you're probably a wordsmith."

Watching me for another moment, she begins speaking out the scene. "Carefully, button-by-button, the gorgeous man removes his shirt. His ab muscles are as hard as steel and scream out for her to touch them, but she doesn't. Instead, she stands silent and waits for his permission as he moves to take off his belt before unbuttoning his pants. He looks at her with a burning intensity in his eyes as if he knows all her secrets but doesn't care. And maybe he doesn't."

"So, Vada. What secrets do you have?" I ask her, wanting

to know, realizing I've spilled my guts tonight, but I haven't learned much more about her than I already know.

"I'm an open book. Other than the trust issues I have. But that's because of all the pricks I've dated in the past. And..." She hesitates. I watch her, completely unsure of what she'll say next. "And from things in my childhood. But it's all in the past now. Without all the liars and cheaters, well I wouldn't be the woman I am today or be able to write strong women in my books. So it all worked out, I suppose."

"Did someone hurt you?" I nearly growl, realizing how territorial that sounded. "I might kill them if you say yes." Just the thought of someone laying a hand on Vada almost sends me into a fury.

"No, nothing like that. More emotional abuse than anything. Being able to trust someone fully is important to me because I tend to go all in when I'm dating someone. The past hasn't been kind to me, that's all I'm saying. Every relationship I've been in has ended badly, so I guess you could say I'm a bit jaded. Empty promises covered with lies, and stupidly, I believed them over and over again. It's probably why I'm *overly* single right now."

"I can understand that. But let me add, I'm an open book too, Vada. I'll always be truthful, even if it hurts. I don't have anything to hide. You know all my secrets." I take a few steps forward and hold her in my arms. Skin against skin and there's something so intimate about standing in nothing but candlelight.

"Get in first," I demand with a smile, watching our shadows dance against the wall.

"So bossy, I *like* it," she purrs, dipping a toe in the warm water, then stepping in, and slowly sitting in the tub. I follow her lead, slipping behind her, my legs holding her in place.

"Ouch, your snake's slithering against my back," she jokes.

"Watch out, you might get bitten," I tell her as I grab a bar of soap and gently wash over her breasts. Vada sinks into my touch, allowing me to put my hands wherever I want.

"The water's so warm, it's relaxing," she states in a dreamy-like tone.

I slip my hands down lower, and my fingers rub against her clit. Letting out a moan that echoes through the bathroom, Vada arches against me, creating more friction. Her head leans against my shoulder, and I devour her mouth with mine as I continue to pleasure her. Dipping a finger inside, I can feel how tight and ready she is for me.

"Fuck, Vada," I whisper in her ear, as she sinks deeper into my touch.

"If you keep doing that, I'm going to lose it," she says between moans.

"Good." With my other hand, I palm her breast, tugging at her nipple that's at full attention.

"God, Ethan." She moans louder, with more intensity in her voice as she places her palms on the porcelain tub, leaning harder into me. Her body tenses against my chest, and she closes her eyes as she allows the release to take over.

"You're so fucking sexy when you come," I whisper against her neck.

She laughs, leaning her head against me. "Didn't realize getting clean could be so dirty."

I take my time, washing her body and hair until she's

completely clean. "You were right about the exclusive treatment. Can I bring you home with me?"

When she mentions leaving, my heart lurches forward. "I wish, Vada. But you'd need a bigger suitcase for me, Henry, and Wilma. My cock and pussy go everywhere with me."

Sitting up, she lets out the cutest laugh ever, causing the water to whoosh in the tub. Considering it's lukewarm and soapy, I take that as our cue to get out and stand. I hand her a towel, and we dry off, and I can't help but admire how beautiful she is, all the way down to her perfect toes.

When I think about her leaving, it just doesn't feel right. Not at all.

And that thought scares the ever living shit out of me.

Grabbing her hand, I lead her down the hallway to my bedroom. "On the bed."

She tilts her head at me but doesn't hesitate.

"How do you want me?" she asks looking over her shoulder.

"You're the guest of the hour; how about you choose." I drop the towel to the floor as she lies on her back. I walk to my bedside table and put on a condom. My dick throbs in my hand and I know this won't take long, but I promise to take my time.

"How's this?" she asks lying on her back, the moonlight casting shadows across the room.

I go to her and start at her feet, kissing her ankles, her legs, the inside of her thighs, until I reach my final destination. As I taste her arousal, she runs her fingers through my hair, letting out moans that sound like music.

"Ethan," she whispers, and my name has never sounded so good. Before she loses herself again, I move closer to her, hovering above her, my dick teasing the outside of her opening. I move slowly, taking my time as our ends meet. She gasps, her eyes closing tight.

"Oh, Vada," I whisper across her neck, and that's the moment I realize we're no longer fucking, but rather, making love. When her eyes open, I know she can feel it, too. The look on her face says it all. Her mouth falls open as I give her everything I have. Eventually, Vada crumbles beneath me, and I follow soon after.

After we clean up, we lie together, both struggling for air, trying to understand what just happened. It wasn't just sex; it was more intense, more emotional. It was like she had opened the Pandora's box that held my heart, pulled it from the shadows, and somehow, it's still beating.

Vada's head falls on my chest, and she's listening to the rapid thump of my heart. I hold her in my arms, trying to enjoy it as much as I can. I know this week is coming to an end, and the truth is, I'm going to miss this. Pulling the blankets over our bodies, I stare out at the moon that's high in the sky from the windows in my bedroom.

"I'd like you to come to the demo and showing at the studio tomorrow. It's from eleven to five. Aunt Millie and Mama will be there, and I'd love for you to be there, too."

She sits up and looks into my eyes. "Really? Like a public thing?"

I nod. "Of course."

"I don't like crowds. They make me nervous as hell," she admits.

"Then hang around Aunt Millie. Crowds don't like her because she's loud and has no filter." I laugh, but it's the truth.

She looks as if she's thinking about it, then gives me a big smile. "You know what, I'd love to go and watch you. I mean, if you really want me there," she says, brushing strands of hair out of her eyes.

"It wouldn't be the same without you. So be my guest of honor?"

She nods. "Of course. Wouldn't miss it for the world."

We lie in silence, tangled together like lovers, and it feels right. My eyes are heavy, and I might fall asleep at any moment because I'm so relaxed and happy. Just as I'm drifting away, I hear Vada say something.

"I'm going to miss this. Seriously," she mumbles softly against my chest.

"Then don't leave," I whisper, holding her just a little tighter. "Stay another week or month or I dunno, forever?"

She sighs, and I know she's halfway between sleep and being awake because the words that leave her lips are completely inaudible.

CHAPTER SEVENTEEN

VADA

GOOD MORNING," Ethan says, handing me a cup of coffee while I'm still lying in his bed. Sitting up, I take it from his hands while trying to pat the hair down on my head because it's all crazy and wild. My eyes are barely open, and I feel like I could sleep for days. After last night, I could probably sleep for weeks, but that wouldn't work because I have a book to finish.

"I've been thinking about something," I admit, clearing my throat with a sip of steaming hot coffee.

"Yeah?" He perks up. "You'll walk around naked the rest of the time you're here?"

I playfully roll my eyes at him. "Not quite, but I *was* thinking about extending my stay."

Ethan takes the cup of coffee from my hand, sets it down on his nightstand, and within two seconds his lips are on mine. I'm moaning against his mouth before he releases me.

"That makes me so damn happy, Vada. You have no idea."

He brushes the outside of his fingers against my cheek then stands and returns my coffee.

"I have to call my neighbor about feeding my cat and get in touch with the airline. Lots of stuff to do in so little time," I tell him, finally feeling awake and taking another sip of coffee. I'm going to need all the caffeine today.

"And you have to come to the studio today to watch the live show." He winks.

"I already told you I wouldn't miss that for the world. Plus, I need to stock up on mugs. I seriously need a hundred of them," I say holding a blue and purple handmade mug in my hand. "I love them so much."

Ethan grins at me proudly, then begins pulling clothes from a drawer and getting dressed. I watch his muscles flex as he puts on a shirt, and all I want to do is tear it off him. The man should walk around shirtless with a body like that, but then again, I'm good with keeping him all to myself.

"You said it starts at eleven, right?" I ask again, confirming.

"Yes, and lasts until five. So anytime today. I just want you to see everything. Maybe you can write it into one of your books one day," he suggests with a wink. I can tell he's in a good mood, and him being so damn happy is contagious.

"Okay, great. I'm going to try to get some words in and then I'll Uber down there." There's so much inspiration in me from last night that I have to get some writing in today, or I'll internally combust.

"I can ask Aunt Millie to pick you up," Ethan insists.

"That's sweet of you. But I have a feeling she'd ask me five thousand questions, and I don't know when I'll be finished with this chapter I'm working on."

BROOKE CUMBERLAND & & LYRA PARISH

He lets out a laugh then walks toward me. Leaning down, he places his hand around the back of my neck and kisses me. "I'll see you there, babe."

"Save me a seat," I tell him, not really sure how this demo thing works.

"I've always got a seat saved for you on my face." He kisses me again, before saying goodbye. Once I've finished my coffee, I slip on my dress and head downstairs. I refill my cup before heading to the cottage to get some words down after I take a shower.

Once I'm dried off, I put on one of my favorite A-line skirts and a tank top, then sit down at my computer and the paragraphs pour from me. The words won't stop coming. It's a high like no other.

I feel like I've ripped my soul open, and though I don't want to jinx myself, this might be the easiest book I've ever written. I've never been this inspired, and I'm pretty sure Ethan is to blame. Actually, I *know* he is.

Hours pass, and I know I've lost track of time again and my coffee has turned cold.

Looking at the time, I realize it's just past one. "Shit," I say aloud, grabbing my phone and scheduling an Uber. As I wait around, I call Nora.

"Oh, so you're alive," she says with a hint of accusation in her tone.

"Wow, no hello or anything? I see how it is." I laugh, used to her attitude. If she didn't act like that, I might actually think there's something wrong.

"Glad to know you weren't chopped up into a million pieces," she says.

"You're so dark and need to lay off those CSI shows. Geez. I'm alive, so there's that. Okay, nice chatting with you!" I kid.

"Not so fast young lady. You left me on a cliffhanger yesterday, so I'm going to need you to go ahead and let me know how the date of the century went."

"Well…" I begin, replaying last night in my head and grinning like an idiot.

Nora clears her throat.

"He was married," I explain.

"Is he still?" Her inflection raises.

"No, no. It's nothing like that. He's a widower, and seriously Nora, I was bawling like a baby. Just think of the saddest movie you've ever seen times a million then put it on crack. Ethan's wife was pregnant and had complications during the birth. The baby was premature and got really sick and didn't make it. They both passed away within two weeks of each other." My voice cracks and I realize I'm choking up.

"I don't know what to say," she mumbles. "That's much heavier than I was expecting."

"Believe me, I know." I suck in a deep breath. "Still, the date was perfect though. The best date I've ever had."

"Well, I'm happy for you." Her tone is raw.

"Thanks, Nora," I say with a smile. "Oh! So that brings me to the point of this call." I look at my phone and realize the Uber is outside, so I rush across the yard and continue the conversation when I get in the car. "I'm going to call the airline and try to reschedule my flight. I'm staying another week. I'm getting ahead with this impending deadline, and I think it would be good for me to utilize the inspiration that's coming to me now while I can." I bite down on my lower lip, thinking of all the ways Ethan can inspire me for the next week. "So I hope you won't mind taking care of Oliver for me for just a little bit longer?" I ask as sweetly as possible.

She sucks in a breath. "I guess." Her tone is unamused, but I know she's just giving me a hard time. She's probably thinking the same thing I am. *Inspiration* equals Ethan's cock.

"Thank you. I owe you. I'm on my way to watch Ethan do a live pottery demo at his studio, so I have to get going. I'll snap some photos though and text them to you."

"Good, because I need to see what this Prince Charming looks like." Her tone perks up, and I know she's not annoyed with watching Oliver another week like she pretends to be.

The Uber slows in front of Paris Pottery & Studio, and I hang up with Nora before thanking the driver. I stand outside and look up at the sign with a whole new perspective, and my heart lurches forward. It's so beautiful that he named the studio after his daughter, knowing it would've made his wife happy. I take in a slow breath as I see all the people packed into the building and try to push my anxiety to the side as I enter.

I move through hordes of women who are all looking in the same direction. From the back of the room, I see Ethan at the wheel, with his hands on the clay, and I can't help but admire him. Honestly, though, I think every woman in here is. He's smiling and explaining his methods as all eyes stay glued to him. He looks so good wearing black dress slacks and a solid, dark gray button-up shirt. His sleeves are rolled up his arms, and his top buttons are undone. He looks business-professional, but I know what's under all of that—eight-pack abs and a pierced cock that knows how to melt off panties.

Weaving my way through, I see Aunt Millie laughing and

speaking loudly in the middle of the room while she brags about her nephew. As soon as she makes eye contact with me, she waves me over, and I feel slightly embarrassed, but I walk toward her anyway.

Ethan's head lifts, and his entire face brightens when he sees me.

"Hi," I mouth, and he winks at me. Women start searching around the room, trying to figure out who he's openly flirting with, and that's when heat hits my cheeks.

"There you are, Vada. Ethan told me you'd be showing up, and I've been waitin' for you. Want you to meet someone," Millie says, grabbing my hand and forcing her way past people.

"Vada, this is my sister, Mollie. Ethan's mama."

My mouth drops open when I see a spitting image of Millie standing in front of me. "I had no idea you were a twin; what a surprise!"

"Mollie, this is Vada, the girl I was telling you about who's staying with Ethan." Millie gives me a wink, and I instantly blush.

"It's so nice to meet you," I tell her, and she gives me a hug, a customary southern greeting I've come to expect.

"You too, honey. I've heard so much about you," she says, and I glance over her shoulder at Millie with a smile and can only imagine what she's said about me.

"Really?" I try not to be too embarrassed.

"Yeah, Millie told me about your books, and I downloaded a few onto my Kindle."

I instantly start stuttering. "I hope you enjoy them." All I can think about are these sweet older ladies reading those raunchy sex scenes.

"I'm sure I will, sweetie," she says, having no idea what she's about to read.

Ethan grabs the bat out of the wheel with a brand-new mug he's just made and hands it to one of the workers who sets it down on one of the shelves.

At that moment, I take a quick photo and send it to Nora. When I look back up, it's like we're the only two people in the crowded room. I can't stop staring at him. It's almost as if he can read my thoughts as his eyes meet mine. Swallowing hard, I snap out of it and feel like a room full of eyes are on me. I can almost feel the jealousy streaming off all the women who came here just to admire Ethan—and not necessarily his work. But it doesn't hurt he's sexy as sin, so I'm sure that's good for business. Although he doesn't need it. His work speaks for itself all on its own.

Once he finishes molding a few more mugs, he goes to the sink and rinses off his hands and arms, then makes a beeline toward me as interns clean up the area and restock his clay. My mouth goes dry when he dips down and gives me a kiss in front of *everyone*. I feel like I'm falling as he completely steals my breath away. Ethan brushes his fingers against my cheek, and before he pulls away, he whispers in my ear. "Hopefully all these thirsty women will get the hint."

I burst out laughing, especially when I get eyerolls from a few ladies staring at us together. "Doubt it. Some look like they're trying real hard and now want to murder me."

He nods. "You have no idea. Oh, did you meet my mama?" Ethan asks, searching around for her. She and Millie are the life of the party on the opposite side of the room. It also helps the interns are serving wine, so many people are giggly and buying mugs like they're shopping with a no limit credit card.

"I have to say I was shocked when I saw two Millie's staring at me."

Ethan chuckles. "I guess I forgot to warn you about that. But trust me when I say Mom is the good cop and Millie is the bad one."

The smile on my face may be permanent. "I'm so proud of you, babe. You've got a full house, and it's all just perfect," I say, sincerely.

"Thanks, sweetheart. That means a lot to me. Really." He places his hand on my cheek and smirks. "Have time to go to the back real quick?" His voice drops low.

"Uhh," I say, as he grabs my hand and leads me away from everyone. We walk down a long hall, and Ethan opens a storage closet full of supplies. He pulls me inside with him, and once he locks the door, we're standing inches apart.

"Fuck, I need you right now," he growls against my lips before he kisses me.

I don't even wait before I'm grabbing at his pants. Ethan takes a step forward until my back is against the only bare wall in the closet. Roughly, he lifts my leg in the air and pushes my skirt up, then tears my panties from my body. The way he's handling me, so desperate with want and need, turns me on even more.

"Shit," he says.

I search his face. "What?"

"No condom," he admits.

"I'm on the pill, Ethan."

At first, he hesitates. So I readjust my skirt back down over my bare ass, and he shakes his head.

"Don't think so, babe." Ethan grabs my ass and lifts me in the air. My legs wrap around his hips as he fucks me against the wall. Small moans escape from my mouth as our tongues swirl together, and I feel so naughty knowing there's a room full of people who suspect something is going on or even hear us.

"Vada," Ethan groans against my mouth. "You feel so good. You always feel so fucking good."

"I want more of you, Ethan. All of you."

He continues to give me everything he can. "When I saw you walk in, all I could think about was this."

"Yes, yes, yes," I whisper, holding on to him for dear life, digging my nails into him harder.

Before I come, Ethan sets me down on the ground and drops to his knees, then pulls my leg over his shoulder. His mouth is in between my legs in seconds. As he devours me, it takes everything I have to hold back all the moans I want to release. He doesn't stop, even when he knows I'm close. I hold onto his arm that's wrapped around my thigh because I feel weak in the knees as I lose myself on his mouth.

"I need more of you," he says, dipping his tongue inside, tasting my orgasm.

"So good," I say between breaths, as he stands, kissing me, allowing me to taste myself on him. He gives me a smirk, then turns me around, and bends me over. I place my hands on the wall, giving me the much-needed support, and arch my ass toward him.

Taking his time, he rubs his rough palms on my ass before

he grabs my hips and slowly slides into me. I gasp as the top of his piercing rubs against me, feeling his length in places he's already been and claimed as his own.

"I'm so fucking happy you're staying," he says as I feel him tense and his warmth fills me. After a moment, I turn around and search his face with a smile, and he kisses me, soft and sweet, pouring himself into me.

"Do you think anyone heard us?" I ask, grabbing a few towels on a shelf to clean us up.

"I hope they all did." He smirks, zipping up his pants, and I roll my eyes.

"Thank you for coming, Vada," he says. "On my mouth."

"So dirty," I say, adjusting my clothes. "Don't you think you should get back? Everyone is probably looking for you."

He tries to straighten his messy hair, and I laugh.

"How do I look?" he asks.

"Like you just had sex. Swollen lips and guilt written all over your face."

He dips down and kisses me again. "Good," he says before opening the door and pulling me out with him.

A few people saw us coming out of the closet, and I'm a bit self-conscious, but I decide to take pride in my walk of shame. We're both adults, enjoying each other's company.

Ethan's hand is leading me as we walk back into the main room and through the crowd. Women look over their shoulders at us and snicker, probably knowing what we were just doing. I'm sure I look as guilty as he does, but he wears it with no fucks given.

Hours pass as I sit in the front row and watch him, completely mesmerized by his amazing skills. Each time he throws me a wink, I playfully roll my eyes at him because I don't want to get shanked when I leave here. Before too long, I realize I need to get back to the house. At Ethan's next break, I tell him I need to leave.

"I understand, babe," he says.

"I still have to call the airline and make arrangements to reschedule my flight, but I'm going to do that once I get back to the house."

Once the Uber arrives, he walks me out and pulls me into his arms. "Bye, babe. I'll see you *very* soon."

"You will," I tell him, placing a quick kiss on his lips before getting into the car.

I wave at him and blow a sweet kiss that he tucks into his pocket before he heads back inside the studio. Letting out a sigh, I decide I want to do something nice for him tonight and ask the Uber driver if he can take me to a grocery store instead. She agrees and drops me off at the door.

"I can wait for you if you'd like," she offers.

"That's okay. I might be a while. Thank you, though," I tell her, and she gives me a wave and drives off.

My phone vibrates, and I see a text from Nora. I guess she figured it out after all.

Nora: DOES HE HAVE AN OLDER SINGLE UNCLE?

I laugh and send her a text back.

Me: No. And your cap locks is on again :)

Nora: DAMMIT.

I swear to myself that when I get back home, I'm going to teach her how to use that damn phone. Laughing at her, I walk inside and grab a cart and go straight for the steaks. As I'm looking at ribeyes and sirloins, trying to decide which one to cook, a tall, Paris blonde woman stands close beside me. She has long, lean legs and a pretty face; the woman could be a model.

As soon as we make eye contact, she flashes a smile. "Oh hey, I recognize you," she says, matter-of-factly, though I've never seen her in my life.

I'm kind of confused. "Really?" I tilt my head, trying to figure out if I recognize her or not.

"Yeah, you were just at Ethan's studio, weren't you?" she asks, her smile never fading, yet her tone is giving off a weird vibe.

I smile back at her, not really wanting to make small talk but decide to be nice. "Oh right. Yeah, I was."

"So I have a somewhat personal question," she tells me, sliding her cart to one side, so we don't block the aisle.

I'm not really sure what to say, so I just nod.

"Are you seeing Ethan? Like, are you two a *thing*?" she asks, her nose wrinkling.

I open my mouth and close it, trying to draw my attention back to grocery shopping. "Something like that, but I'm sorry, who are you?"

"I'm Harmony. It's nice to meet you," she says in an overly sweet tone that sounds fake as she holds out her hand, but I don't take it. "Anyway, I know you're not from around here, so I thought I'd give you a warning about him."

I furrow my brows and look at her like she's lost her damn mind, but still, I'm intrigued to hear what she has to say. I already know about his past and secrets, about his wife and daughter; what else could she possibly have to tell me?

"He likes to make women think he's falling in love with them, especially ones who are just in town on vacation. He makes them believe that they're different from anyone else he's ever been with." My brows raise, shocked by her bold statements.

"You're lying." The words blurt out of my mouth before I can stop them.

She looks at me with pity before continuing. "He has the same MO on all of them, honey. Takes them out on *special* dates to the beach where he'll hold your hand, and you'll walk along the sand barefoot together. He'll bring a blanket for you both to sit on, and that's when he spills his guts to you, just to hook you in even more. Then, once he's gotten his fix of you, he drops you like a bad habit, as if you and he never happened. He'll make you believe you're something special, that he's falling hard, and can't get enough before moving on to the next. Then you're left to pick up the pieces of your broken heart."

I feel sick. My head is spinning because she just replayed the most intimate part of our date. There's no way she could know that. We weren't even in town. The only person I told was Nora, and I doubt he'd tell anyone outside of Aunt Millie. How the hell does she know all the details? I instantly feel like a fool, and my heart hurts.

She carefully studies me, twitching her lips as if she's happy with my response, before she continues. "He told you all about his late wife and baby down at the beach, didn't he?" she asks when she notices all the blood rushing out of my face. "That's his pity game, darling. He knows women can't resist him, but once he makes them think he's going all in, they become putty in his hands." She flashes a genuine, apologetic smile. "Hook, line, and sinker," she confirms, and I wish she'd just stop talking so I can process her words.

Ethan's avoided relationships for years, but I know that doesn't mean he hasn't had one-night stands or flings. Why would he need to manipulate them when he's the one who doesn't want anything more than a physical relationship? But then again, how would she know about our date on the beach and him sharing those intimate details with me? What if it really is his MO? Questions swirl around in my mind, but I can't make sense of them. Nothing is making sense, yet I feel my insides twisting.

Finally, I clear my throat and speak. "How do you know all this?"

"Because I've been in your shoes, hon. So have many other women in town. Once the news started to get around of his dating rituals and women were onto his scam, he moved to tourists only, which is no secret why he rents out the cottage." She purses her lips as if it should all be clicking in my head right about now. "Same old story, too. He says he only does one-night stands to make us feel like we're something special, but once he's bored, we're kicked to the curb." Her expression is firm as if she's warned others before. "I know it's none of my business, but I just felt like you should know. We women have to stay together, ya know? But you can do whatever you want. I just wouldn't feel right walking away and not giving you a warning, since, by the look on your face, no one else has."

I don't even reply or give her a chance to continue again before I walk away without my cart. As quickly as I can, I find a bathroom and close myself in a stall, and that's when the tears unleash. Is that all this is to him? *A game*? Was I stupid enough to believe someone like Ethan could really fall for someone like me, especially when he dates women who look like Harmony? Every trust issue I've had in the past surfaces full force as I think about how easy I let a guy like Ethan in. *What the hell was I thinking?*

Looking down at my phone, I see my hand shaking. Slowly, I'm crumbling and feel like everything I thought I knew was a lie.

I'm a fool.

I should've never trusted him so easily.

He made me believe he was different and that letting my guard down wouldn't come back to bite me, but it looks as if I was wrong. *Again.*

I'm drowning in emotions as I schedule another Uber to take me back to the cottage.

My heart is shattering into a million pieces, and I'm pissed off that I put myself in this situation once again. That bad boy type has always been bad for me, and I realize I was the stupid girl who fell for the same old re-spun lies.

I need to leave.

I need to pack my shit and get the hell out of here as soon as possible.

CHAPTER EIGHTEEN

ETHAN

AFTER I HELP clean up the studio, I hug and thank Millie and Mama for all their support in this venture of mine.

"I really like your *friend*, Ethan," Mama says with a twinkle in her eye, and it's the first time she's really given her approval for a lady since Alana. It makes my smile grow even bigger.

"She's cute. Perfect for you. Seems real nice," she adds, smiling. I know she's being sincere, too.

"She is, but tell me what you think about her once you've read her book, the one Aunt Millie made you download." I laugh, knowing it's probably full of dirty, vulgar sex scenes, especially if Vada's words are anything like the Vada I know in bed.

Millie bursts out into evil laughter. After standing for a little while longer, we exchange big hugs then I walk them out to the car, making sure they leave safely.

"We had a record day in sales," Hilary says excitedly when

I walk back in. I round the counter, and she points her finger to the screen, showing me the amount.

"That's great news. I can't wait to make the donation to the March of Dimes," I tell her with a smile. If there's a premature baby out there that has a fighting chance, I want to do everything I can to save a life and someone else from going through what I did. Jessica, who's in charge of scheduling and other maintenance, lets out a loud aww, but I try to ignore it. I don't do it for recognition. I do it to make a difference, as small as it may be.

"Do you need anything else before I head out?" I ask, trying to change the subject.

Several interns speak up all at once saying they've got it, and I know they do.

"Fine," I tell them with a smile and a wave before I leave for the day.

On the drive home, all I can think about is seeing Vada again, kissing Vada, being with Vada. My thoughts are consumed with her. She's on my mind every moment of the day, and when she's away, it's like a part of me is missing. That woman somehow stole a piece of my heart, and I don't want it back. Hell, she can keep it as long as she's here in Charleston with me.

I drive across town and replay the last week, and I'm so fucking happy Vada is extending her stay. We'll have more time to be together and see where this leads. In my heart, I know this is the real deal, but I need to make sure we haven't rushed into something crazy. Regardless, I'm already falling hard for her, and there's no rescue mission in place. Truthfully, I don't want to be saved. Just the thought of her smile, laugh, the way she says my name, or the look on her face when she loses herself with me, makes me feel things I haven't in a long-ass time.

Before I head home, I stop and pick up a dozen red roses and a bottle of Cabernet, since I know it's her favorite. There's a lot of celebrating to be done since my Vada is staying. Eventually, she'll have to leave, but hopefully only to pack her apartment and return back to me.

Tonight, I want to order in and spend the rest of the night showing her what she truly means to me. At the studio, when she walked in, it was like everything around me had faded to black, except her. Vada makes me feel something I never knew I'd feel again — whole.

When I park the car, my heart lurches forward, and I'm so damn excited to finally be home. It was the longest drive ever. I walk through the house, hurry and feed Wilma, then go through the back door with the roses and wine in hand. The smile on my face almost immediately fades when I see all the lights are off in the cottage and the door is locked. Thinking that she's probably trying to surprise me, I walk back to the house and immediately climb the stairs to my bedroom. Opening the door, I realize she's not there either.

"Vada?" I finally call her name.

I wait but don't hear a reply.

Going back downstairs, I set the flowers and wine down, and that's when I see a handwritten note on the counter.

Confused, I pick it up and read the scribbled words. With each sentence, I feel like I'm choking.

My heart is torn as I write this, but I'm leaving for Chicago tonight. By the time you get home, I'm sure I'll already be on the plane. After I left the studio today, I realized how stupid I was being. I can't be here, Ethan. I won't be played, and I won't allow myself to be that girl. It's better this way. -Vada

I notice the splashes of ink on the paper and know she was crying as she wrote this, and it tears me apart. Immediately, I pull my phone from my pocket and call her, but it goes straight to voicemail.

My voice cracks when I speak. "Vada, please call me. I don't know what you're talking about or what happened since you left the studio. Please talk to me so we can figure this out."

I know I sound desperate, but the best thing that's happened to me in a long time just walked away with a half-ass explanation, and I need to know what triggered this. Everything was absolutely perfect when she left the studio. I think about the last words we exchanged, and it was goodbyes, surrounded by smiles. If I would've known she'd be leaving for good, I would've never let her get in that car earlier. Something happened, and I'm going to lose my mind until I know what.

Halfway hoping this is some sick joke, I walk back to the cottage with the key tightly grasped in my hand and almost lose it when I see all of her belongings are gone. Her suitcase, laptop, everything. It's as if it was all a dream and she never happened.

"No," I say, quietly to myself. "This isn't happening."

Instead of giving up, I keep calling her, hoping she'll answer, but she never does. After everything we've been through, after I ripped my heart open and poured myself out to her, she leaves me. Vada saw my true, raw self, and she still left, and the thought of what I've lost cripples me.

It's been a week since Vada left, and it's like my whole world has shattered into shards again. She rejects my calls and sends me straight to voicemail. I'm pretty sure I'm blocked at this point because I've called and texted so much, begging her to talk to me. Regardless of what I say on those voice messages, she doesn't return them. I have zero control over this, and while I'm trying to be patient and give her time if that's what she needs, it's not in my nature, especially when I'm hurting so badly.

There's a hole in my heart, and I miss her so fucking much.

"Why don't you go to her?" Millie asks as we drive across town to pick up some plants for her front porch. She refused to let me stay home and wallow in my emotions and even pulled the old people card to force me to join her.

"Because she doesn't answer my calls, so why would she want to see me? All I want is an explanation of what the hell happened, some clarity on what changed from the time she left the studio to when she decided to bail. Everything was going so great, then she was gone." I ball my hands in fists, and I feel like I'm losing all the control I'd found when she was here.

"Tell me what the note said again," she insists. "Maybe I can read between the lines."

I repeat the note without even having to look at it because I've read it so many times and have the damn thing memorized. Millie sits silently while she thinks and parks the car.

"Something significant enough to make her change her mind must've happened after she left the studio. That's what you need to figure out," she tells me matter-of-factly as if I hadn't already been trying to put the pieces together. I've been driving myself insane thinking of different things, but nothing makes sense.

I roll my eyes as I unbuckle, then mumble more to myself as I get out of the car. "Leave it to detective Millie."

Not waiting for me, she grabs a cart and walks inside the store. This is the last thing I wish I were doing right now, especially considering I'm in such a pissy mood. By the time I find Millie, she's looking at an ugly bush and talking to someone who's even uglier—Harmony Hansen—an ex-fling I'd rather forget about.

"Oh, hey Ethan," she says in an over-the-top, high-pitched voice. "So nice seeing you last weekend at the studio."

"Yeah," is all I offer, and Millie elbows me in the ribs for being rude, but things didn't end well between us, and I'm not going to give her false hope by being polite.

Harmony knew the rules between us. One night, that was it, but she didn't get the hint until I kicked her out of bed the same night. From that point on, she's desperately tried to get back in bed with me, but I knew what she wanted and what I wanted were two different things. I wasn't ready for anything serious, but she made it very clear she wanted something long-term. *A husband.* I was in no emotional mindset for that. Though it's been years, she hasn't given up on the thought of us.

Harmony is literally the epitome of stalker ex. After one night, she was *obsessed*. If I could go back in time, I'd erase the history between us. It was a stupid, liquor-influenced mistake.

"Don't mind him, hon. He's in a bad mood. So what have you been up to lately?" Millie genuinely asks. "Haven't seen you at the book club meetings in a while." I really have no reason to stay around, so I pretend to look at plants, hoping this isn't a long conversation.

Millie talks about the books she's been reading and mentions Vada's name. My heart sinks at the thought of her.

"Vada, right," she says as if saying her name is venom. "I ran into her at the grocery store after I left the studio last weekend. Real sweet girl," Harmony says, plastering the biggest deviant smile on her face.

I blink, realization setting in. "Wait. What did you say? When did you speak to her?" My jaw clenches, and I instantly realize what happened. No telling what Harmony told Vada, considering I ignored her at the restaurant the night of mine and Vada's date. It was easier to pretend she didn't exist when she looked at me from across the room with those come-hither eyes. Seeing me with a woman always drives her insane, but seeing me with the *same* woman at the studio probably set her off even more.

"Oh, nothing." Harmony realizes how much she fucked up by saying those words. She knew exactly what she was doing when she saw Vada. She was trying to sabotage what we had.

Millie notices my flaring nostrils and speaks for me. "So what did you two discuss, hon? Her books?"

After hesitating for an awkward moment, she gives me an evil smile. "Ethan."

BROOKE CUMBERLAND & & LYRA PARISH

"You *bitch*," I growl, anticipating Millie's reaction, but she doesn't scold me like I figured. Instead, she glares at Harmony and shakes her head before walking away without another word, leaving the two of us alone. Aunt Millie and the silent treatment together is a frightening pair.

Before walking away, I look Harmony dead in her eyes. My tone is serious, and I hope for once she gets the fucking hint. "I told you once before we'd never be anything, so get the fuck out of my life and stay out."

Millie is still shaking her head as she pushes her cart forward, leaving me alone with her.

"Ethan, baby. I didn't tell her anything she wouldn't have eventually figured out." Her words are laced in a condescending tone. "It was just too easy. It was obvious you two were getting close and it was easy to assume you were telling her all about your sad past. Once I saw you take her down to the beach on your little date, there was no way you hadn't told her and as soon as I brought it up, her face dropped faster than her panties could for you."

"Don't you fucking talk about her that way," I growl, taking a step toward her and giving no shits how loud I'm being.

She doesn't even flinch, her cold stone glare fuels my anger even more. "Too bad she left before you could lie your way out of this one." She flashes an evil grin before jerking her cart forward and walking away.

My blood is boiling at the revelation of what just happened. As soon as I saw Harmony at the restaurant, I should've left and taken Vada somewhere else, but I didn't want to start our night on a bad note. Should've figured she'd watch us the entire time.

I inhale deeply before glancing around for Aunt Millie and jogging to catch up to her.

"I warned you about those random dates, Ethan. Those type of women are no good and now look what happened," she scolds.

Pinching the bridge of my nose with my fingers, I sigh. "I know. I wish I could take back *that* mistake. I'm beyond pissed about this. I don't even know what to do right now. No telling exactly what Harmony said to her, although I have a pretty good guess considering what she just told me. She's a goddamn liar and a jealous and petty bitch." I shake my head, growing angrier at the whole situation.

"Language, Ethan," she reminds me.

I follow Millie to the counter and pay for her plants then help her load them in the backseat of her car. After we get in and before she starts the engine, she turns and looks at me.

"You know what you have to do, hon. You're a fighter. You always have been and always will be. When you want something, you go after it. So, fight for what you love. Harmony was wrong to do that to you, and I'm going to have a chat with her Mama the next time I see her."

I give her a small smile. Millie may be a polite, southern woman, but that doesn't mean she doesn't have a dark side. She doesn't get back—she gets even—especially for her favorite nephew.

"So, I'll take care of things while you go to Chicago," she adds, trying to cheer me up.

"I don't know, Aunt Millie. What if it can't be repaired?

Who knows what Vada thinks of me now, and I know I couldn't handle losing her all over again. I don't think I can get over her or ever will. Maybe she needs some space, and I'll give that to her, even if it kills me in the end." The words hurt coming out, but once you lose someone you love, you're constantly afraid you'll lose it again.

"Don't be stupid, boy," she slaps me with her harsh words. "You fight for her and don't stop until she listens to you. Harmony filled her head with lies, and you need to clear the air, even if she decides she doesn't want to be with you. You owe her that much at least."

God. Leave it to Aunt Millie to put me in my place.

Although she's right, Vada may not give me the opportunity to clear the air—so I'll have to go another route to grab her attention.

CHAPTER NINETEEN

VADA

ONE YEAR LATER...

MEMORIES INVADE my mind as I walk past all the tourists on King Street.

I've been excited, anxious, nervous—*everything*—since I found out one of my book tour stops was in Charleston. My publisher arranged the schedule, and there was no changing it, although I wasn't completely sure I would've wanted to. However, being back is bringing a mixture of feelings, and I don't know what to make of them.

Especially with the way I left—the last time I saw Ethan.

I've heard his voice, but we haven't talked since that last day I was here.

Leaving Charleston in tears doesn't give this city the best feeling of returning, but I'm not running away. At least, not yet.

It'd be impossible to forget a guy like Ethan, especially

when my latest novel was primarily inspired by him. As cliché as it sounds, he really did bring something out of me that had been missing all this time. My writer's block was gone, and I couldn't get the words out fast enough.

Who knew my week with Ethan Rochester would lead to writing the best novel of my life?

When I returned home, I couldn't write because I was so hurt and upset. But eventually, anytime I thought about Ethan and our time together, which seemed to be all the time, my inspiration fire would reignite. I tried to push away all the negative thoughts and only focus on the good that happened between us. It was the best week of my life until I ran into that witch of a woman, and she ruined everything. My trust had been broken, and I was too scared to start over, not knowing the difference between his truths and her lies. It was too much.

As soon as I presented the new book idea to my agent, she ate it up. The novel practically wrote itself, which, as a full-time writer, I can confidently say has never happened to me before. Once I finished the first draft, relief rushed through my veins. My agent insisted my characters get a full happily-ever-after, even if I didn't.

So of course, they did. Complete with a big southern wedding and lots of babies.

Ethan had done what he promised all along—helped me find my writing inspiration. It's safe to say it wasn't the southern air or lifestyle—it was all him.

Our story ended with my heart broken and me crying in the plane bathroom. I knew the moment I told Nora, she'd tell me to talk to him and find out what happened. And if what Harmony said was true, she'd say to give him a piece of my mind. Hell, she was ready to fly to Charleston and do it for me like the mama bear she is.

Suffice it to say, I didn't do either of those things. Everything from my past resurfaced, and it was the same issues and lies from all my failed relationships all over again. Fear, self-doubt, depression. It all kept me from making that step, from going back to Ethan.

He'd called and texted dozens of times. They were all left unheard and unread. I was being childish, and I knew that, but I couldn't bear to hear if everything Harmony said was actually true. I couldn't bear to hear him lie to me either. I needed more time to think, and I had major deadlines to worry about on top of that.

Until one night, I finally braved listening his voicemails. It took two bottles of wine, of course.

The sound of his voice crippled me. God, it was so sexy when he spoke, but I could hear the pain in his tone. It was evident, yet I couldn't bring myself to hit the call back button. I was pathetic and weak, I knew that.

In the beginning of his messages, he desperately begged me to tell him why I left and what happened. Those messages broke me down. I was the spitting image of Carrie Bradshaw crying in her wedding dress—except I was alone with an empty glass of wine and my cat.

Later, his messages changed because he had found out about Harmony and knew she'd said something to me. He pleaded with me to tell him what she said so he'd know how to fix it, but that was the thing. It couldn't be fixed. Even if her words were complete lies, the fact that I let a guy like him affect me in only a week scared the shit out of me, and a part of me was running. Running from the reality of what happened so quickly. I'd become too vulnerable, and it was a hard lesson in trusting another guy with my heart. The pain made it impossible for me to move forward.

Part of me wanted to go back to him, hear what he had to say, and fall back into our easy ways. However, the logical part of me knew it was a formula for disaster. My life is in Chicago and his is in South Carolina. We both knew this; yet he didn't give up.

After one bottle of wine was emptied, I continued to the other, listening to another handful of his messages. God, they made me hate myself. I wallowed in guilt and self-sabotage. Yet, I continued to convince myself that staying away was for the best. It'd be better to get over him now before I really fell hard because if it didn't work out the second time around, my heart would be destroyed beyond repair.

I lied to myself, even if I didn't want to admit I was. Eventually, I started believing those lies.

Nora's words from earlier repeated in my head. *Give the boy something, Vada. Whether it's an explanation for your silence or just to say you want him to stop calling, give him some kind of closure.*

I knew she was right, but I couldn't work up the courage. Until I'd emptied those two bottles of wine and that's when I finally hit the call back button.

He didn't answer, of course. It was well after two in the morning, which meant it was even later where he was.

The next morning, I woke with the worst headache of my life. I rarely drank, and when I did, it was one or two glasses max. I was certainly paying for it now.

A loud knock echoed through my apartment, and I

groaned, unable to deal with anyone or anything. It was well into the afternoon, so it could only be Nora.

"Use your key," I hollered, hoping my words would make it to the front of my apartment. After a moment, the knocking continued. "Dammit, Nora," I grumbled, pulling myself from the bed and opening the front door.

"Miss Collins?" an older man's voice rang.

Blinking, I finally lifted my head and saw he was holding a large vase of red roses.

"Yes?"

"Floral delivery, miss. Here you go." He handed them to me with a smile.

"Oh, um, thank you."

"My pleasure, miss. Have a great day."

After closing the door with my foot, I walked the vase of flowers to my kitchen and set them down. Searching for a card, I found one after my vision cleared.

To Vada,

I miss you more than I can express, but I'm willing to give you space if that's what you need to think everything through. I'll wait for you until you're ready.

You know where to find me when you are.

-Ethan

P.S. Don't think I won't stop reminding you how much I care and miss you though.

P.S.S. Hope you're feeling okay this morning. Take an Ibuprofen and drink lots of water. Hangovers are the worst.

"What?" I gasped aloud. I racked my brain, saw the empty

wine bottles on my living room floor, and reached for my phone. I checked my calls, and that's when realization hit.

I called him nine times last night. Left him voicemail after voicemail, worst—*drunk voicemails.*

"Oh my God," I murmured. "Fuck."

Why in the world would he even want to talk or see me again after that? I probably mentioned his cock and how I wished I could fuck his brains out just to use him the way I felt used. *Oh my God.* This was fucking awful.

After telling Nora the story, she laughed her ass off. Completely at my expense, of course. She even said she heard me rambling through the walls, and when I cursed her out for not trying to stop me, she said it was for my own good.

One thing I know for sure is that I told him I needed space, which was true. It was why I didn't respond to his messages because I knew the minute I did, I'd throw everything out the door. I needed to stay focused, work on my novel, and not let a man chase away my dreams.

Space was good. He knew writing was important to me and respecting that made me fall for him even harder.

After that night, I stayed on track and kept writing. His calls and text messages stopped, but the flower deliveries didn't.

Every week like clockwork, a new bouquet showed up at my door. Every week, a new note.

I miss you, Vada.

You're beautiful. Just thought I'd remind you.

I'll wait for you. No matter what.

I was tempted to call him several times, but I didn't want to lead him on. Truthfully, I didn't know what I wanted. I hated to cause him more pain, not knowing if I'd ever be able to be who or what he needed. Space and time couldn't heal everything, and there was no guarantee when that would even be.

"You'll always have a deadline, Vada. Go to him," Nora insisted.

If I was being a hundred percent honest with myself, it was fear keeping me from making that step.

Fear of putting my heart back on the line.

Fear of losing my creativeness.

Fear of giving it all up for him.

Fear that I wouldn't be able to trust him even if he'd given me no reason not to.

Even after a year, I kept all the dried rose petals from dozens of flowers that sat in a box on my nightstand. I looked at them every day and tried to remember the way he smelled. He always smelled so damn good. Purely male mixed with a hint of amber. It was heaven.

Even though I essentially ignored him for months, he refused to let me forget him, as if I could. One note he sent hit me hard. It said he was giving me all the space I needed, knowing I was working on my book, and that he'd be there when I was ready. He wasn't giving up—no matter what.

Part of me wondered how long he was going to keep it up and if he was still thinking of me as much as I was thinking of him.

Then the flowers stopped coming a month ago. Right after the book's release.

First, a week went by, and I didn't think much of it. I'd been preparing for my book tour, but when another three weeks went by, I knew I'd run out of time. A million thoughts tumbled through my mind. Had he finally gotten over me? Did he meet someone else? Was he done trying? Had I fucked up by not giving him some kind of response that wasn't wine-induced?

Or worse. Did he see the book and now hate me for it, for sharing those intimate parts of our relationship?

I knew the only person I could blame was myself and admitting that brought more pain than anything else. I was heartbroken all over again, and it was my own damn fault.

"Vada!" Olivia, my new assistant shouts. She's been traveling with me and helping keep my schedule straight. The promotional tour for this new book is the biggest and longest I've ever done, so my agent suggested bringing someone to help me. Considering there'd be a lot of events and meetings to keep track of, I took her advice and went through an agency to find a highly-qualified assistant.

Blinking, I realize she's waving her hand in front of my face. "You need more caffeine," she mutters, pointing to the Styrofoam coffee cup on the table, silently telling me to chug it down.

"I'm fine," I finally reply, grabbing for the cup anyway. She catches me daydreaming all the time, so I know she's used to me zoning out on our conversations. "What is it?" I ask before taking a large sip.

"Which outfit do you want to wear?" She's holding up a dress in each hand. "You have the brunch meet-n-greet at eleven and then the signing from one to four."

I narrow my eyes, studying each one. They both work just

fine, but being in Charleston has me thinking I could maybe—
just *maybe*—see Ethan. As quickly as the thought enters, I push
it back out.

"The navy blue one," I say, pointing to the one in her right
hand. "With my cream-colored heels."

"Great." She hangs them up. "You can wear your new
blazer over it for dinner."

"Dinner?" I rack my brain, but I can't remember.

"Yes. You have an intimate meet-n-greet from six to eight."

I put it in my mental calendar, although I know I'll forget.
Every day of this tour has me so jam-packed that I have a hard
time keeping track.

"Thank God you have a great memory." I sigh.

She turns around before grabbing something and walking
toward me. With a loud plop, she tosses a fat notebook on
the table.

"I have a great planner," she corrects. "This is your Bible."

I arch a brow, amused by her dramatics. "The Bible?"

"Yes, the Bible." She starts petting it. "Treat it as such,
anyway. It has everything in here from your schedule, your
coffee orders, your outfit options for each event, your flight
itineraries, your sleep schedule." She pauses to blink up at me.
"Everything."

"Jesus, Liv." I pull it toward me and start flipping through
pages. "Surprised it doesn't have my menstrual cycle in here."

"Page twenty-two," she says, not missing a beat. I look up
at her with an arched brow, and she winks. "You think I just
know when to pack extra chocolate and pads?" She taps her
temple with a finger. "My number one job—keep my author
happy."

I smile. "Wow, I never realized how much you do behind the scenes. Thank you."

She blushes, and I know our little moment is over. "Okay, well you have twelve minutes to finish your breakfast." She gives me a pointed look that tells me I better eat.

Grabbing the planner off the table, she walks back to her makeshift office in the opposite corner of the hotel suite while I finish my breakfast.

Exactly twelve minutes later, Olivia is pushing me into the shower and reminding me to shave my legs.

I look down and realize she's right.

"How did you—" I shout from behind the curtain.

"The Bible!" she yells back, and I smile.

Less than two hours later, we're heading to one of the hotel's meeting rooms where a group of readers are waiting for me. No matter how many events I do, it still feels surreal. I'm completely humbled that people read my words and even want to meet me. It's an intoxicating feeling, and every time I leave one of these events, I have to pinch myself because this is my life.

"You have one hour and forty-five minutes, and then we have to get you to the bookstore for the signing. Ready?" Olivia asks as she brushes one of my flyaway hairs off my forehead. She really is my right-hand woman.

"Absolutely!" I say, confidently and smile.

She opens the doors for me, and I'm greeted by a dozen women who all smile and start clapping as soon as I walk in. It's so overwhelming, yet I can't deny how great it feels. They stand up from the table, so I can give them each a hug while they introduce themselves to me.

Meet-n-greets are intimate and personal, which is one of the reasons I love them so much. I meet a lot of readers online, but there's nothing like connecting with them in person.

Once we're all seated and settled with our plates of food, questions start flying. "So does Nathan know you wrote a novel about him?" Amelia, a woman around the same age as me, asks. "I mean, he'd have to, right?"

Everyone leans over the table, itching closer to hear my response.

The *New York Times* reached out to my publisher and requested an interview with me and printed it right before the book's release where I confirmed the rumors about this novel being inspired by true events. Considering this was a steamy romance novel, they were intrigued, along with thousands of readers. So, of course, the million-dollar question everyone wants to know—did "Nathan" know I wrote this book primarily based on our week together?

Of course, Nathan was *actually* Ethan, but I haven't confirmed whether or not he knew because honestly, I didn't. I had no idea if he followed my social media pages, but I haven't come out and told him personally. Hell, I haven't even spoken to him. Concern on how readers will react to that truth is why I haven't publicly revealed that. Part of me worries my readers would be upset if I told our story without his permission, and the other part of me stresses they wouldn't connect with the characters if they knew the real-life love story didn't end the same.

"I don't think so," is all I offer to Amelia.

"Do you think he'd be mad if he found out?" another

woman asks. "Like now that the book is released, he could know, right?" There's hopefulness in her tone.

"Sure, he could. Not sure he follows romance books, but never say never," I say with a forced smile. I knew going on tour and having these meet-n-greets would bring up uncomfortable questions and memories of Ethan, but being in the same town as him and where the story took place is affecting me in more ways than one.

The brunch ends on a high note when I announce there'll be more standalone books in the series. My agent ended up getting me a three-book deal for the series once she sold the first one, and after I sent in summaries for books two and three.

"You did good," Olivia praises. "I am starting to wonder if this Nathan guy is real though." She flashes me a wink, and I roll my eyes.

"Sometimes I wonder the same thing," I say with a chuckle.

"The more you talk about him, the more he sounds too good to be true."

"If it sounds too good to be true, it probably is," I say, confirming what she already expected. Ethan's the full package, and anyone that meets him would probably agree. However, that doesn't void the fact that we were destined to end this way.

His emotional baggage mixed with my trust issues was a disaster waiting to happen. But I can confidently say that if I had to do it all over again, I undoubtedly would.

The afternoon and night go by fast. The signing is a huge success and meeting readers who want my autograph and picture has me floating on cloud nine. I'm not a social person by nature, but as soon as I enter that room filled with people whose eyes are all on me, something in my brain switches.

I'm suddenly the most social person ever, remembering to smile and hug people. I pose for pictures and thank them for coming. Nora calls it Vada 2.0.

I laugh, thinking back to the conversation. She knows how introverted I am and often teases me for all the food deliveries I get.

"You have more men coming and going from your apartment than the Playboy mansion," she mocked.

"Well, what can I say? Food is my weakness." I smirked, earning a groan from her.

"One of these days, I'm teaching you to cook a damn meal for yourself. How are you ever going to be able to cook dinner for your future husband?"

I gave her a look that told her that wasn't something I'd have to be concerned about anytime soon.

"You could go out every once in a while. Meet up with some friends," she encouraged.

"I don't have friends." I deadpanned. "Except you and Oliver."

"Oliver and I don't count, although I don't appreciate you putting me in the same category as your damn cat." She grunted. "I mean, real friends. Girlfriends the same age as you. Go out and have fun. You're always worried about the next deadline."

"Because I'm always on a deadline." I half-laughed, half-cried because it's the truth. Deadlines on deadlines. "Plus, I don't want to be that social anyway."

"How's it you can't socialize with people your own age, yet you go on tour and socialize with hundreds of strangers?"

I shrugged with a grin. "One of life's many mysteries I guess." I flashed a smug smile.

"It's like you have an alternate personality. Vada 2.0."

I laughed, rolling my head back because I'd never thought about it like that.

"You're absolutely right, Nora. But Vada OG is my comfort zone."

Considering my writing schedule and hectic lifestyle, cooking just isn't a priority right now. Neither is going out and socializing. I know I'll probably look back one day and wished I'd formed some close friendships, but people who don't read or write just don't understand the passion. I'm better off in my own bubble with online friends who share the same interests and night owl schedule.

"Okay, that's it for the day," Olivia says with a deep breath. "You're officially off-duty."

"I can finally take off these heels then." I sigh with a choked laugh. "My writer's uniform is so much better."

"Wearing the same clothes for a week isn't a uniform, Vada. It's right up there next to homelessness." She eyes me, daring me to challenge her. "Plus, you look *good* in a dress and heels. You should go out and show yourself off." Her eyes light up at her suggestion.

"Sorry, Vada 2.0 is officially down for the night. Plus, I should get some writing done tonight. My agent is already clawing at me for the next part."

Sighing, she nods, and we head toward the doors and walk out together. Charleston is beautiful this time of year; a warm breeze blows across us as the sun starts to set. I close my eyes briefly, letting all the memories soak in.

"You okay?" she asks, adjusting her purse on her shoulder.

I blink and inhale a deep breath. "Yeah. I'm good." I smile wide.

Stepping out onto the sidewalk, Olivia plays on her phone, and just as we round a corner, I hear someone calling my name.

"Vada!"

The voice is deep and recognizable.

Spinning around, my eyes search for him, and it doesn't take me long to spot him. His hands are shoved into the front pockets of his dark-washed jeans. Dark shaggy hair tamed to one side. Piercings in both ears. Scruffy jawline.

He's as gorgeous as I remember. Every bad boy stigma.

A single girl's wet dream.

Ethan.

CHAPTER TWENTY

ETHAN

IT'S BEEN a year since I've seen Vada in the flesh, but she's just as stunningly beautiful as I remember. Her hair is a tad longer, but thick and just as gorgeous as before. Seeing her in a dress instantly starts doing things to me, but when I see the expression on her face the moment her eyes find mine, I know the feelings I had for her haven't wavered a bit.

Coming here was a risk. After sending her forty-five flower bouquets and never getting a response from her, I didn't know if she'd want to see me or not. However, when I heard she would be in Charleston, I couldn't pass up the opportunity to know once and for all if we still had a chance at making this work.

I haven't stopped thinking about her since she left. I've been a tortured soul since the moment she walked out of my life, and I haven't even looked at another woman since she's been gone. This was my last attempt to lay it all out there on the line.

"Ethan," she says, her tone soft, as she walks toward me. I see the surprise in her eyes and hope I'm not breaking the rules by coming here.

"Hey." I meet her halfway, unsure how to approach her. I try to read her body language, but she isn't giving much away.

"You're here," she says simply, almost as if she'd been anticipating seeing me, which makes me hopeful. She releases a breath, and I wonder if it'd be appropriate to hug her.

"Of course, I am," is all I say in return.

"I'm just surprised to see you here. I just got the feeling you were done waiting." I don't miss the hint of sadness in her tone.

I take another step toward her. "Oh fuck no."

My blunt words take her off guard, but she chuckles softly anyway.

"I wasn't sure I'd ever see you again."

"I wasn't sure you'd ever want to see me again," I admit. "After everything that happened with Harmony and your writing deadlines, but seeing as you didn't slap me across the face, I take it you don't hate me." I rock back on my feet, nervously.

She smiles, lowering her eyes to hide the blush that sweeps across her cheeks. "Well, I actually decided to stop hating you yesterday. So, good timing."

"Whew, glad I waited."

We both smile.

"So...what are you doing here, Ethan?" She sucks in her lower lip as she studies me.

"I came to see if you got my flowers," I tease, knowing damn well she did. I paid good money to make sure they were delivered directly to her.

"Um, ya know…I'm pretty sure I did." She puts a finger to her lips as if she's truly thinking about it.

I narrow my eyes, but she cracks a smile, giving me the reassurance I need.

"Of course, I did," she finally confesses. "They were all really gorgeous," she says sincerely, and the nerves begin to wash away. "However, it was quite ironic, don't you think?" Her lips tilt up in a mock grin.

"Why do you say that?" I narrow my eyes.

"I recall you specifically telling me you weren't a 'sending flowers' type of guy." She flashes a wide smile, knowing damn well she's right. "And yet, you sent me a bouquet every week for almost a year."

I run my hand along my jawline, covering up the guilty smirk that flashes across my face. "To be fair, I hadn't been that guy for years, so I didn't want you to have the wrong expectations." I pause, keeping my eyes locked on hers. "But meeting you changed everything."

"Well, thank you. I loved them all."

"You're welcome." I smile in return. "I wanted to make sure you always had fresh flowers to keep you inspired. I would've sent Henry, knowing how much you enjoyed his company, but I was worried you'd send him back in a bucket."

She bursts out laughing, and it eases everything inside me.

"I can honestly say I don't miss your cock chasing me." She pinches her lips together, preventing her from smiling.

"Well, that's really a shame, because he's sure missed you," I tell her sincerely.

"I bet he's had plenty of other visitors to attack."

Lowering my eyes, I shake my head. "I haven't rented the cottage out since you left."

"Oh." Her voice sounds surprised, although she really shouldn't be. I haven't wanted anyone else in there. To me, it'll always be hers.

Clearing my throat, I work up the courage to tell her why I'm really here. "I came for you, Vada." I look into her big green eyes. "I haven't stopped thinking about you. I couldn't miss the opportunity to finally see you."

She bites on her lower lip before popping it back out. "How'd you know I'd be in town?"

"Aunt Millie saw it in the paper and told me," I confirm. "She's your biggest fan now." I smile. "Once I found out, I thought about this moment over and over and decided that even if you were pissed to see me, I had to chance it."

She pauses a moment before smiling with a nod. "Well, I'm glad you did," she replies, her words taking me by surprise. "I've wondered what it'd be like to see you again."

"Yeah, it's…" I pause, unable to stop looking at her lips and thinking about the way she tastes. Screw formalities. "Fuck, Vada. I'm sorry." I step toward her.

"You don't have to—" she begins, but I'm quick to cut her off.

"That's not what I'm apologizing for." I'm quick to close the gap between us, wrap my hand around her neck, and pull her lips to mine. I kiss the fuck out of her and am relieved when she kisses me back.

A risk—to assume she'd want to kiss me—but one *so* worth it.

Her tongue dances with mine as her hands wrap around my

waist and pull at the fabric of my shirt, desperate to deepen the kiss. My palms cup her cheeks and hold her closely. The world spins around us as if we're the only two people here, and in this moment, it's only Vada and me.

"I've missed you so fucking much," I breathe against her lips, leaning back just enough to whisper the words. "Did you miss me?" I bravely ask, needing to hear her say it.

She swallows then nods. "Yes, but—"

"But it's not enough," I finish for her, predicting her thoughts.

"We live completely different lives," she confirms.

"That's not a good enough reason to be apart, Vada."

"You stopped sending the flowers," she whispers. "I thought you were done waiting for me and the thought nearly sent me back to desperate levels." I furrow my brows in question. "Wine," she clarifies.

Brushing my finger along her jawline, I tilt her chin to look back up at me. "I stopped sending them because I knew you'd be on tour. I sent them because I wanted to give you the space and time, knowing you needed it, but without smothering you. I wanted you to know that I was still thinking about you and that I'd wait for you as long as you needed me to—as long as I knew there was still a chance for us."

"Oh, I didn't think of that," she says, chewing on her lip again. I can see how nervous she is to be around me. "Harmony's words really stung and affected me, and it made me really scared at how fast I was falling for you. Then I started second-guessing everything."

"I'm so sorry about her. Everything she told you was based on lies, and I'm sorry she put them in your head, but I can't undo that part of my life. As much as I wish I could." I groan, getting fired up just thinking about her and the shit she pulled.

"I know, and I wanted to believe you once I finally listened to your messages, but it felt like it was too late. I'd already left heartbroken, and I knew I wouldn't survive another broken heart if I called you back or even returned. It felt inevitable that things would eventually end, so I knew it was for the best to stay away."

"How could you make that decision without actually talking to me first?" I ask, more anger in my tone than I'd meant. "You weren't the only one hurting and confused, Vada."

She swallows, her body tensing. "I know, but I felt like I couldn't trust you even if what she told me was a lie. I couldn't trust those feelings anymore, and I couldn't go through the pain all over again."

"I never lied to you, Vada. You had no reason not to trust me," I tell her.

"I don't trust easily," she reminds me. "I didn't know if the feelings I had for you were real either because they formed so fast. I'd hoped once I was back home and writing, I would get over you."

"And did you?" I ask, brushing strands of her hair behind her ear, feeling the goose bumps along her skin.

Her body stills as she thinks about her answer. "No," she says just above a whisper. "Not even close." I bring her mouth back to mine, feverishly kissing her.

"Thank fuck," I murmur against her lips. "I've been dying to kiss you for twelve long months. I was going to die if I had to hold back."

She laughs against my mouth and the sound sends tingles

down my body. Her laugh is music to my soul, and it's the first true smile I've had in months.

"How inappropriate would it be to ask you to have dinner with me tonight?"

She chews her bottom lip as if she's really thinking about it. "Depends. Are you going to offer your cock to me again?"

"Henry?" My brows lift. "I knew you missed him." I smirk at all the memories of him chasing and scaring the shit out of her.

She chuckles again then shakes her head. "No, not *that* cock."

I choke on my words before I can even spit them out. "Shit. You're still as feisty as I remember."

Her lips spread into a wide, knowing grin. "C'mon, Casanova. Take me to your lair."

After Vada introduces her assistant to me and explains she'll be riding with me, we take off in my car. The woman looked at me like I was a figment of her imagination.

"Are you sure you didn't mean to say *riding me* instead?" Holding her hand as I drive back to my house, I press her knuckles to my lips as we fall right back into our old rhythm. "Or are you two not that close?" I flash her a cocky grin.

"Ha! Still as confident and arrogant as *I* remember." She squeezes her hand in mine. "Quite the opposite actually. She probably knows more about me than I do. She takes care of my schedule and everything, down to what underwear I wear that day."

"Really?" I arch a brow in her direction before sliding the material of her dress up her thigh and revealing red, lacy panties. "Remind me to send her a thank-you card."

She bursts out laughing. "Please don't. She'll take it to heart and frame it or something."

Once we arrive at the house, I study Vada's features, and I'm positive memories of us here together are flooding through her mind. She looks around, her face contorting into something unrecognizable.

"What's on your mind?" I ask once we're standing on the sidewalk in front of the house. Grabbing her hand, I pull her body toward mine. "I'm really happy you're here."

"It feels a little like déjà vu," she says, honestly. "And it scares me a little."

"Don't be scared, sweetheart." I press a soft kiss against her mouth. "I don't bite, unless requested of course."

"Why can't I get you out of my head, Ethan Rochester?" She tilts her head as she asks the question. "You're bad news."

"Probably because I'm the best sex you've ever had," I say, confidently.

Her eyes widen as the realization hits her. "Oh my God." She covers a hand over her mouth, laughing. "You read the book."

"Of course, I did." I smile in return. "It was the church's book club pick of the month. Very popular with the older ladies, by the way."

Her cheeks redden, and her eyes bug out in embarrassment. "Stop it!"

"I'm serious! I couldn't look Aunt Millie in the eyes for

weeks once she learned of my cock piercing." I chuckle, shaking my head at the memory of her reading those parts.

Her face falls into her palms as she dies laughing. "Guess they read between the lines."

"Yeah, Nathan?" I quirk a brow.

She's still laughing. "Fuck. I honestly didn't think you'd even hear about it."

"Seriously? It's been in the local papers for weeks and in those 'anticipated reads' articles. Apparently, being with the bad boy excites a lot of people." I wink.

"Aunt Millie must think I'm a slut," she blurts out as I lead her down the path to the front of the house.

"No, but she thinks I'm a manwhore. So thanks for that," I tease, taking out my keys and unlocking the door.

"She thought that long before I came around." She laughs.

"True."

After walking into the house, I lead her into the kitchen and pin her against the wall. I know I should be taking it slow with her, considering we still have so much to discuss, but I can't pass up this opportunity. I have no idea what it'll lead to —if anything at all—and I've been miserably waiting for this day to come.

"What do you say we skip dinner and go right to dessert?" I ask against her neck, inhaling her sweet scent.

I feel her chest moving rapidly as she breathlessly responds, "*Yes.*" It's a whispered plea, and I don't waste any time. My lips on hers, her hands on me, our bodies pressed together as if we'll float away without the weight of the other.

"Tell me what you want, Vada," I murmur in her ear.

"You."

Wrapping my arms around her hips, I dig my nails into her ass and squeeze. Lifting her up, she circles her legs around me, and I carry her to the table.

"I can't wait any longer, I have to taste you." After setting her down, I kneel and part her legs just enough for my hand to slide up her leg and tug at her panties. "Red is officially my new favorite color." I smirk, looking up at her as she blushes.

Sliding her panties all the way down, I pull off her heels and toss them aside. "When I'm done devouring you for dessert, I want you bent over this table wearing only those heels."

"Oh my God…" She moans, leaning back on her elbows. "You're giving me way too much book material." She smiles, and I know she's not joking.

"I'd be happy to give you more inspiration…I have all night, sweetheart." I meet her eyes and wink before parting her legs farther. Hooking her knee over my shoulder, I kiss a line until I reach the sweetness in between her legs. "Goddammit, Vada," I growl, flattening my tongue against her slit. "I've been craving this for months. Fuck."

She releases a throaty moan as I find her clit and circle it with my tongue. Her fingers wrap around my biceps, and her nails dig in as I slide inside her.

"Vada…" I breathe out, desperately.

"Ethan…" she whimpers in return.

I bring my hand up her thigh and rub the pad of my thumb along her clit as I kiss along her inner thigh. My fingers slide down her pussy and push inside her tight cunt. Her hips buck at the intrusion, and she bellows out another moan.

"Do you know how fucking mad at you I was when you left

me, Vada…" I slip a second finger inside her. She stretches her neck and looks at me with hooded eyes. I push in deeper. "I lost my shit when I realized you were really gone. Your luggage was gone. The drawers in the cottage were empty. You took the last sliver of hope I felt and ripped it to fucking shreds." I increase the pace, finger fucking her hard and fast.

"Ethan…" she begins, but she bites her bottom lip, and a moan slips through them.

"I called and texted you a hundred times. For the first time in years, I felt something. I hadn't realized it until you left, and my heart broke all over again."

"Ethan, stop talking…" she orders, and I spread her legs wider and sink in deeper. The more I think about it now, the angrier I get, knowing she could've called or texted me so we could've worked it out. I still would've given her space to finish her book, but I was left in limbo.

"Aunt Millie told me to go to you. She said to fight for you, Vada. I wanted to, tried to convince myself I should, but I couldn't bear the thought of you telling me to leave or that the feelings were no longer mutual. So I fucking chickened out. Sent you flowers instead. Tried telling myself it was for the best, that one week with you was enough."

"Ethan, please…" she begs, her eyes filling with tears.

I slow my rhythm but don't stop.

"I've been lying to myself for twelve fucking months, hoping you'd realize how much you meant to me and come back to me, but now that I have you here with me, all I want is for you to know how much you hurt me…"

"Ethan…" She begs louder. "I'm sorry!" I rotate my wrist and slide my finger in and out of her again. "Fuck. I'm sorry I left without saying goodbye. It's been torturing me ever since." Her honest words fuel my anger even more.

"Then why didn't you come back sooner and let me explain?" I fire back. "I needed you as much as you needed me."

She winces before her body tenses, and I feel her tighten around me. Her orgasm starts to build, and she's no longer in control as she arches her back and releases a deep, desperate moan. Desperate for more, desperate for me.

"I was scared," she finally admits. "I'm still scared."

Standing up, I push my fingers inside my mouth and taste her sweetness.

"Don't be, because, for the first time in six years, I'm not. I know exactly what I want."

She adjusts her body and sits up so she can look up into my eyes. Reaching for me, she wraps her petite hands in mine. "Isn't getting closure this time a much better ending to our story?"

"This isn't the end, baby. We're just beginning."

CHAPTER TWENTY-ONE

VADA

THE MOMENT his lips touched mine, I was transported back to the first time we kissed. He tasted so good and memories of our week together were front and center in my head. I'd been anticipating this moment, wondering if it'd ever happen, and now that it has, I'm more scared than ever.

"Vada..." he says my name in a pleading drawl. "Please tell me you want this as much as I do."

I do. I want it so bad.

"I don't want to hurt you again, Ethan," I say, softly. "I don't know what I can offer you."

"You." He presses his lips against mine again, silently pleading for me to give us a chance. "I only need you."

I release a moan as our bodies press together and his hand wraps around my neck and holds us there, waiting for my response.

"Say yes, Vada..." he begs as his mouth brushes against mine. "Let me love you."

God. This man was the full package, and I'd be a fool to walk away from him again. No guy has ever fought this hard for me and knowing he waited a year for me lets me know how serious he is about us, too. After a moment, I finally nod, giving him the approval he needs.

"Thank fuck," he mutters against my lips before taking my mouth. He positions my body between his legs and kisses the hell out of me. My heels dig into his ass as he rubs his fingers over my hard nipples.

Without warning, he scoops me up and carries me down the hall. I squeal with a laugh and cling to him while he takes us upstairs. I know exactly where we're going, and the smile on my face never falters.

Once we're inside his bedroom, he kicks the door shut and flashes me an evil grin.

"I've imagined this for a long time," I admit because it's the truth. I've spent many times in my bed, getting off to thoughts of him.

"Yeah?" He sets me down on the bed, towering over me with hope in his eyes. His mouth lands on my collarbone before he brushes his lips along my exposed shoulder.

Deciding to mess with him first, I reply in all seriousness, "I want to use a strap-on and fuck you in the ass while stroking your dick until you come."

He immediately chokes and leans back to face me, reading my expression. "Just because Nathan's into that, doesn't mean I am."

I burst out laughing. "Dammit. You really did read the book."

Smiling, he presses his lips back to mine. "Of course. Several times."

I wrap my arms and legs around him, pressing his body to mine. "Several times?"

"Yup. Memorized it like the fucking Bible."

"Had I known you were going to read it, I wouldn't have gone into such grave detail about your cock," I tease, loving the way his body feels pressed to mine.

"Speaking of which, Henry's butt hurt that you gave him a chick name."

My head falls back, laughing, which I seem to be doing a lot around him. "I'll explain to him that it was for his privacy, and hopefully. he'll forgive me."

"I'm sure you two can work out a deal." He winks, sending butterflies straight to my core.

Leaning back, his hands push up my dress until he's pulling it over my head, and I watch as he tosses it to the floor. His eyes widen as he stares at my bra, which happens to match the red, lacy panties I was wearing.

"I think your assistant needs a raise." He smirks, rubbing the pad of his thumb against my nipple.

"I can dress myself, you know. She just so happened to pack everything for this trip so I could work on edits."

"Another book?" His brows raise, intrigued.

I nod. "There's always another book."

"Does Nathan make an appearance in it?" He kneels back slightly to remove his shirt. My eyes trace down his chest and abs, wandering all the way down to his happy trail that leads right to *my* happy place.

"He doesn't, but don't worry, Nathan will always be my

number one." I flash him a wink as I reach over and help him unbutton his jeans.

"Good. Now let me fuck you like in chapter thirteen, because I'm in the mood for some backdoor adventures." He grins, waiting for my reaction.

"Nice try, Casanova." I unzip his jeans.

"A man can dream." He shrugs, standing and removing the rest of his clothing.

I swallow as I take in his beautiful body. "Well, keep dreaming."

"I think I am," he says, genuinely, kneeling between my legs again and brushing his fingers along my cheek. "I still can't believe you're really here."

"Me either."

He presses his lips to mine, sweet and slow, then slides his tongue in just enough to part my lips. My hands hang around his hips before my fingertips trail along his deep V line that brings me to his erection, hard and solid. I'd be lying if I said I hadn't missed the feel of his cock, the way it tastes, the way it filled me so fucking deep, and that piercing.

I feel the warmth of his hands wrap around my body and unhook my bra. He slides it down my arms and tosses it, cupping my breasts and massaging my nipples with his fingertips. I groan at the contact, loving the way his hands feel on me.

"I told myself once I finally had you back in my bed, I'd take my time with you, but fuck, baby. I don't think I can." He groans, moving his lips along my jaw and neck.

"We have all night," I remind him. "I need you as much as you need me."

"Fucking hell," he growls, leaning back as he grabs the back of my knees and pulls me to the edge of the bed until my ass nearly hangs off.

I squeal, grasping onto his arms. My head falls back with laughter at his urgency. "You make me so horngry," he says with a devilish grin.

"Horngry?" I ask, amused. "What's that?"

"It's when I can't decide if I wanna fuck you or eat you first." The corner of his lips tilts up in a knowing smile.

I laugh as he brings his mouth to my pussy and sinks his tongue inside.

"Guess I know which one won," I say.

"Yeah, I decided to spend some quality time between your legs first."

Sinking a finger inside, his tongue circles my clit and works me up until I explode. I barely recover when he flips me over and takes me from behind.

His hand wraps around my neck, tilting my head back so he can stare into my eyes as I unravel around his length. I love the way he's looking at me as if he can't get enough of my body.

"Vada, *fuck*." He groans, pushing into me deeper and harder. "You feel so fucking good. So tight and wet, baby."

He pulls back slightly, the tip of his piercing rubbing against my pussy. God, I missed that piercing. Pushing back in, he increases his pace and sinks deep into me until I explode again. Fuck, he's so good at that.

Fisting my hair, he pulls my head back again until our lips collide. He continues his rhythm, fucking me so good and hard, I can barely keep up with my breathing. I feel his body tense, his kiss deepens, and then he moans against my mouth as he releases inside me.

"Vada..." he whispers after a minute, against my lips, so soft and sweet.

"Yes?"

"Stay with me," he pleads, running his tongue along my bottom lip. "Give us a second chance."

He kisses me before I can respond, which gives me the time I need to process his words.

"I have three more weeks of my promo tour," I begin to explain as he arches his hips.

"Baby, I've been waiting twelve long months for you. I can wait another three weeks as long as I know you'll come back to me."

His words send shivers down my spine because they're everything right and perfect; any girl would die to hear them.

"I want to..." I start, unsure of how to answer him.

"Then do. Take a leap of faith, Vada. I'm not like those other douchebags you've dated. I won't hurt you," he pleads with such promise, and I want to believe them with every fiber of my being.

Before I can respond, he pulls out of me and lies down on the bed next to me. I turn my body, so we're facing each other, and he moves closer until our chests press together.

Cupping my cheeks, he stares directly into my eyes. "Vada, baby. I'm not proposing marriage here. I'm asking you to give us a second-chance at making this work. I gave you space because I knew you needed it till you finished your novel, but I'm only a man of so much patience. I can't keep putting my heart on the line if you aren't willing to meet me halfway."

His confession hits me like a ton of bricks. This man is too good to be true, and I'd be a fool to run away from him again.

My eyes begin to water because his words are so strikingly beautiful. No man has ever fought for me and definitely not this hard. I want to savor everything.

"How would we make this work? I live in Chicago," I remind him.

He gives me a look that says it's not a good enough reason, and deep down in my heart I know it's not. "Yes, and last I checked, you're a writer, who can literally do her job anywhere."

I swallow, realizing all the excuses I'm making.

"Vada, what is it? Tell me," he asks, noticing my hesitation.

"If I moved here, to be with you, it'd put a lot of pressure on us to make it work. I already have a mile-long list of relationship and anxiety issues. I don't know how it'd work with that kind of pressure on us."

"There'd be no pressure, babe. I know writing is important to you, and I have my pottery, so I'd never put you in a position to choose one over the other."

"Okay…" I finally respond with a nod, giving him the reassurance he needs.

Enthusiastically, he grabs my face, and our mouths collide together. I laugh against his lips at his eagerness, and he smiles in return.

"As long as Henry doesn't try to eat Oliver." I grin, weaving our legs together.

He presses a long kiss on my lips. "No promises." Winking, he pulls me off the bed and starts leading us down the hall, and before I can question what he's doing, he brings us to the bathroom.

"Showers just haven't been the same without you." The corner of his lips tilt as he runs the water.

"You know? I've been thinking the exact same thing." I grin, letting him lead me inside.

"Good, because I plan to make up for lost time." He pins me to the wall as the water cascades down on us. His fingers find their way to my pussy while I stroke his shaft. He wastes no time hooking my leg around his waist as he slides back inside me. "I don't know how I ever lived without this — without you — and now that I have it back, I'm not letting you go."

I love his possessive side, even when he's being overly sweet about it.

He fucks me into oblivion, my breaths coming out in heavy pants. I dig my nails into his arms, holding onto him for support as he rips me in two.

Every part of me tightens as another wave of pleasure surrounds me.

"God, I'm so fucking close," he mutters against my neck as my hand tangles in his hair. "But I want to be inside you all the damn time, every single minute possible. How's it I can't get enough of you?"

"I thought a lot about this over the past year," I admit.

"Oh yeah?" I feel him smile against me. "Did you think of me when you touched yourself? Did you get off on those thoughts?"

"Well, you read the book," I tease.

"Ah, yes. Chapters two, three, six, and fourteen," he responds without missing a single beat.

I chuckle, amused he really did memorize the damn book.

"Chapter six was my favorite, I think. The way you screamed so hard during your orgasm, you ended up taking a lamp out."

"Oh my God." I blush, laughing at him. "To be fair, the lamp wasn't supposed to be there."

Without replying, he pulls out, turns me around and pins my chest to the shower wall.

"Chapter thirteen," I blurt out.

"What?" He leans his head over my shoulder almost as if he needs clarifying he heard me correctly. "Are you sure?"

I look over my shoulder and grin widely. "Absolutely."

His eyes widen before scraping his teeth along my shoulder. "Fuck, Vada. You're trying to fucking ruin me tonight, aren't you?"

"Only in the best way possible."

I feel his cock press against the small of my back. Shaking my ass, he drags the tip up and down my cheeks before positioning himself against my opening. He moves the showerhead so it's not directly on us before leaning back and pressing a hand on my spine till my back is arched enough for him.

He takes me by surprise when he kneels down, spreads my legs, and starts stroking his tongue along my slit. "Relax, Vada," he demands, soothing his hands along my hip. "Do you trust me?" he asks, and I don't hesitate to nod because I do. I really do.

He slides a finger into my tight hole as his tongue works my clit. My body relaxes against his touch, although the feeling is foreign. He loosens me up until he thinks I'm ready and when he stands back up, he slowly eases inside me. At first, it's so tight, and the pressure is so uncomfortable, I'm not sure how I feel about it. Then he slides in a bit more and wraps a hand around my waist, holding me in place.

"Touch yourself, baby. It'll help you relax, so you don't tense up," he tells me, and I oblige.

Sliding a hand between my legs, I rub my clit and feel the buildup as he slides in some more.

"Holy fuck," I blurt out at the intense sensation. I'd never felt anything like it.

"You feel so goddamn good, Vada. Fuck, I won't be able to last much longer."

A few moments later, my orgasm builds and everything tenses.

"Vada! *Fuck*, oh my God," his strained voice echoes through the shower as his climax hits him hard.

Breathless, we stand under the water together, both sated and defeated. He spins me around and captures me with a kiss.

"If you can still walk after that, then we're not finished."

CHAPTER TWENTY-TWO

ETHAN

I CAN'T REMEMBER a time where I ever felt the undeniable hunger to have someone as much as I crave Vada. There's an animalistic desire I can't ever seem to satisfy. Prior to Vada, those thoughts would've never crossed my mind, but now, that thought no longer scares me.

"I'm pretty sure my legs will fall off if I try walking right now."

Smiling, I reach for the soap and reposition the showerhead over us.

"Let me clean you up then." I wink, lathering the soap between my palms before carefully placing them over her soft skin. She moans at the contact, and her head falls to the side.

I cover every inch of her perfect body and gently rinse her off. Although compared to what we just did, this somehow seems more intimate. After leading her out of the shower and drying her off, I carry her back into my bed and tuck her under the covers.

"I have a confession to make," I say as I slide into bed next to her.

"Oh yeah?" She looks up at me with hooded eyes. "What's that, Casanova?"

"I didn't really invite you over for dinner." I grin.

She turns and leans up on her elbow. "Well, then I guess I also have a confession."

My brows raise.

"I already had dinner when you invited me over for dinner." She smiles, and it's the cutest fucking thing ever.

"Ahh…I knew it." Flashing a victorious smile, I wrap my arms around her and hold her. We lie like that for several moments, both clinging to each other as if we'll die without it.

"I know you didn't ask, but I just want you to know something."

She angles her head up toward me and waits.

"I haven't been with anyone since you left. Haven't *wanted* to be with anyone. In fact, Wilma's pissed she wasn't the only pussy I had in here, but once she calmed down and I explained everything to her, she got over it," I confess with a grin.

Vada wrinkles her nose and snorts. "Wilma gave me the stink eye the last time I was here, so she probably thought I was taking over her territory."

"Yeah, she's a territorial bitch, but she'll have to get used to sharing now." I wink.

"Maybe Oliver and her will hit it off," she says with fake amusement.

"Well, if Oliver loves pussy as much as I do, then I'd say he'll warm right up to her."

"Oh my God!" She grabs the pillow that's against the headboard and throws it directly at me. "You're so bad."

"Yes, but you love it," I say without thinking. Worried she'll analyze those words, I open my mouth to say something else, but she cuts me off before I can.

"I do," she says softly, but looking directly into my eyes. "Who knew I would?" She smirks, lowering her eyes as a blush forms on her cheeks.

"Well, I can't say I'm really surprised. I mean, I'm a catch."

"I swear to God," she says, laughing and throwing another pillow at me.

Finding her tickle spot, I dig my nails under her arms then laugh as she squirms against me. She squeals and tells me to stop, but I can't get enough of this. Enough of her. Laughing and smiling. She's so fucking perfect.

"Ethan, please...I'm going to pee if you don't stop!" She's giggling, and before I know it, I pull her face to mine and kiss the fuck out of her.

"I can't let you leave without telling you first." I inhale briefly, rubbing the pad of my thumb along her bottom lip. "I'm so in love with you, Vada Collins. I think I always have been, but having you back in my life, falling right back into our ways as if no time has passed, solidifies everything I've felt for you." I pause, studying her expression before continuing. "I love you."

She sucks in her lower lip, her eyes widening as she swallows and processes everything I've just said.

"Why are you so good to me, Ethan? I mean, seriously. I leave without saying goodbye, I drunk call you and leave you a bunch of crazy voicemails, you send me weekly flowers, and when you find out I'm going to be back in town, you don't let the opportunity slip by to see me."

Her words come off accusing, but I know they aren't meant to be.

"I told you. I'm a catch." I wink.

"Stop." She chuckles. "And now you've just told me the most beautiful thing in the world, and I'm still so terrified to repeat them, although I want to."

I brush the hair away from her face, staring into her eyes. "I didn't say those words because I expected you to say them back. I said them because I never thought I could love anyone after Alana—I never allowed myself to—but with you, I want to. It was freeing, finally feeling like it's okay to love someone else."

"You have no idea how much that means to me." She grabs my face and plants a deep kiss on my lips. "Seriously." She kisses me again. "You just melted all my fears away, Ethan Rochester."

The next morning comes too fast, and soon we're standing on the front porch, saying goodbye. We spent all night wrapped in each other's arms and talking. I also spent some time studying certain parts of her, and though neither of us got much sleep—because I wasn't about to waste the short amount of time I had with her sleeping—we were up bright and early drinking coffee and eating breakfast together like tradition.

"Come back to me," I whisper against her lips, gripping her cheeks between my palms.

"I will," she whispers back. "I promise."

Closing my eyes, I try to get ahold of my emotions before kissing her once more. Olivia came in an Uber to pick her up, and in Vada's words, "to make sure I actually get in the car" since they have another flight to catch.

I walk her to the door, and when Vada opens it, I pop my head in and smile at her assistant. "Hello, again." I flash my million-dollar smile.

"H-hi," Olivia stumbles, clearly blushing.

"You're just mean," Vada teases, reaching up to give me one last hug.

"I was saying hi," I defend. "It's called being polite down here in the south," I remind her, teasingly.

"Yeah, right…" She rolls her eyes. "With your shirt off."

I shrug, smirking.

"Text me after you land, okay? Or call me. Or just stay, I mean, whatever."

She chuckles before giving me one last peck on the lips. "I will."

As I watch them drive away, it feels like a knife drives directly into my heart. *I know this isn't the end; she'll be back; we'll get our second chance to do this right*, at least those are the words I tell myself.

~

"What's wrong with you?"

I spin around in my chair to Aunt Millie standing in the doorway of the tower.

"You scared the shit out of me," I say, releasing my foot off the accelerator and stopping the pottery wheel. I dip my hands in the bucket of water and quickly wipe them off.

"Watch your language," she scolds, giving me pointed look.

"Sorry, Aunt Millie. What are you doing here?"

"What am I doing here?" she asks as if she's offended. "Well, boy, if you ever answered your dang phone, I wouldn't have had to leave my church group early to come check on you."

Guilt surfaces and I feel awful for making her worry. "Sorry, I've been working."

"Yeah, I see that." She looks around the tower and eyes the stocked shelves with mugs that are ready to be glazed. "You've been working 'round the clock again?" She arches a brow, and I know that look.

"Yes, but I'm just trying to keep myself busy," I tell her, which is the truth.

Ever since Vada left a week ago, I think about her nonstop and the anxiousness to have her back drives me crazy. Drowning myself in work is the only way to keep myself sane.

"That doesn't mean you ignore my phone calls." She clucks her tongue.

"You're right. Well, I'm fine. Just working to keep my mind busy."

She flashes me one of her pity looks, which I fucking hate. "She'll be back in a couple weeks," she reminds me as if I don't already know that. "So while I'm glad you aren't wallowing around, I need to get you out of this house."

"I've been out," I retort, though she knows it's only a half-truth.

BROOKE CUMBERLAND & & LYRA PARISH

"To the studio is not going *out*. C'mon. Get cleaned up and dressed. You're taking me to the church dinner tonight."

Smiling, I nod.

I'd been working so much, I filled up every ounce of space on my shelves, which meant I had to start glazing them so I could put them in the kiln next. I loved every step of the process, but glazing was something I could do without much thought. Creatively, I just did what felt right for that piece, and no two were the same.

Per Aunt Millie's request, I cleaned up and dressed so I could take her to the monthly church dinner. It was good to get out of the house for a change, but just another reminder that I was missing my other half. I told Mama and Millie about her return and anticipated permanent return, yet they refused to allow me to stay cooped up while I waited for that moment.

"Oh, did you hear?" Katie, a girl I've known since kindergarten, leans over her chair.

"Hear what?" I ask, turning to face her. Her eyes widen as she licks her lips, and I know it must be something juicy.

"Harmony was caught having an affair with one of her daddy's best friends, and he cut her off, *completely*." Her eyes widen with a smirk on her face. "No more fancy clothes, expensive car, and getting her hair done every week."

"What a pity." I snort. "Guess she'll have to start hustling for her next sugar daddy."

"Well rumor has it she caught one of those STD's, so unless her sugar daddy doesn't mind double-wrapping every time, I doubt she'll find one who'll want to take care of her."

I choke back a laugh at her words but realize it's funny as hell.

"Well, karma's a bitch when you get caught fucking a married man," I say, not feeling the least bit of pity for her. It'd been a long time coming for karma to catch up to Harmony and her antics.

"The best part? The guy's wife had suspected something for quite some time and hid one of those nanny cams in their bedroom, so she got the entire show on camera." She arches a brow with a knowing grin. Yeah, that'll be somehow "leaked" out.

I leave the church dinner in a much better mood than when I arrived. Seeing familiar faces definitely helped.

"Thanks for dragging me out, Aunt Millie," I say, kissing her cheek before opening the car door.

"You're very welcome. Now stop ignoring my phone calls, so I don't have to do it again." She winks, and I nod.

Once I'm back inside the house, I'm not the least bit tired. I decide to walk around the back. Henry greets me out there as I wander around the garden and cottage. It's been quiet out here ever since guests stopped staying, which was probably for the best given my state of mind during those months.

Getting a new idea, I pull my key out and open the cottage door. I've only been in here to keep up with the dusting and cleaning, but now that I'm looking at it in a whole new light, I decide it could use a makeover. Something that'll actually get some use.

And when I think of Vada, I get the best idea yet.

CHAPTER TWENTY-THREE

VADA

"V ADA !" I hear Olivia calling my name, but I roll over and ignore it, pleading for just ten more minutes of sleep. "Vada, I know you can hear me." Her tone is accusing and harsh.

"Go away," I mumble, covering my head with the pillow.

"You cannot just lie in bed all morning," she tells me, but I beg to differ. I'm exhausted and she being in here isn't helping.

"Yes, I can," I retort. "I'll skip breakfast and shower in a half hour. Now turn off the light."

"Nice try." I feel her rustling around, and soon the covers are whipped off me.

"Hey!" I shriek, quickly trying to cover myself up, but she's too fast. "I could've been naked under here."

"Considering you're on the phone until three a.m., I'm actually surprised you aren't."

"Ha-ha," I mock. "I was too tired for phone sex last night, so the joke's on you."

"Yeah, clearly." She rolls her eyes. "Now c'mon. You need to stay on your schedule." She slaps my ass, and I shriek.

"Okay, God. I'm up." I sit up and stretch against the headboard.

"Good. Another flower bouquet was delivered this morning." She points to the vase of red and white roses. "You two are sickening, by the way."

I burst out laughing, smiling at the gorgeous view. Sliding out of bed, I walk to the table they're on and pull out the card.

To my Vada,

When I think about what the future holds for us, I grin like an absolute idiot. But then again, how could I not when I know you're the One.

Good luck today — you're going to kill it!

Love you,

Ethan

I press the card to my chest and sigh.

"We get it," Olivia's words snap me out of my dreamy haze as she yanks the card out of my fingers and sets it back down. "Breakfast. Shower. Dress. *Go.*"

I pout and scowl at her for ruining my moment. Girl needs to get laid or something. Geez.

My publisher has arranged for a podcast interview this morning and then another meet-n-greet before the book signing later this afternoon. It's another busy day, but I don't mind. The busier, the better so I can keep my mind occupied.

Ethan's been sending me flowers to every hotel we stay at

since I left a couple weeks ago. He sends them with the sweetest of notes, too, and I find myself anxiously waiting for them. They're the only thing connecting us right now when the phone calls and text messages aren't enough.

Though the thought of uprooting everything I've ever known in Chicago still gives me anxiety, I know I'll only be happy being with Ethan. I haven't quite broken the news to Nora yet, which is something I need to do before it's too late.

Once the day is over and I'm back in my hotel room, I decide it's now or never.

Grabbing for my phone, I think about what I'm going to say before calling her.

"Your stupid cat got hair all over my favorite sweater," she says immediately when picking up the call.

"Oliver doesn't shed," I protest. "Are you sure it wasn't a different cat?"

"You think I have a parade of cats around here or something? It was yours," she says matter-of-factly. I grin, knowing she secretly loves Oliver as much as I do.

"Well, I'm sure he's very sorry. Plus, it's not really his fault. I'm sure you were picking him up and loving on him, and that's how he got hair on you."

"I would never," she retorts.

I laugh, but we both know the truth. "I'm sorry. I've been a little busier than usual. When I get back, I'll make sure he gets brushed each day, so he doesn't shed as much, or you could brush him?"

She huffs into the phone. "Now you want me to spend quality time with him? Oliver loves to play hard to get when I try to catch him, probably learned it from his mama."

I chuckle, shaking my head at her though she can't see me. "If only I had a camera in my apartment. I bet you two are the best of pals."

She grumbles.

"So how are things going? Where are you now?" she asks, changing the subject.

"Texas," I reply. "It's humid as fuck, too."

"Yeah, us northerners can't handle that kind of heat. Aren't you glad you'll be home in just a week? It's starting to get chilly here finally."

"Well, that's what I kind of wanted to talk to you about."

"You're not leaving me with this damn cat," she immediately blurts outs.

"No." I laugh. "Ethan asked me to stay in Charleston with him," I say the words aloud for the first time, which surprisingly doesn't give me as much anxiety as I thought. I told her the story of seeing Ethan and how we were talking again but hadn't gone into detail about the status of our relationship.

"Oh," is all she offers.

"Yeah."

"So, you'd be moving down there," she says the words as if she's ripping off a Band-Aid.

"I think so," I say softly. "I mean, that'd be the only way to know if a relationship between us could really work. The long-distance would always cause problems, so—"

"Well about damn time," she says, bluntly.

"What?" I ask, laughing. "What do you mean?"

"You've been pining after that boy for a whole damn year, and now that you've reconnected, you'd be a fool to not see where it can go. There's nothing up here for you, Vada," she reminds me, though Chicago is all I've ever known.

"But the thought of just packing everything up and moving for him worries me because what if—"

"What if, what?" she cuts me off. "What if it doesn't work out? But what if it does? Or what if you never take the risk and know for sure?" She fires out the questions as if she's challenging me to really come up with a response.

"But—"

"Vada, dear. Don't end up like me."

"What's that mean?" I ask, pulling my brows together.

"I missed out on the greatest love of my life, and now I'm in my sixties alone babysitting some ugly cat."

I chuckle at her admission. "What happened?"

"Well, back before smart phones and sexting," she begins, making me laugh even harder that she knows what *sexting* is. "I met a man in college who I fell in love with, and although we were madly in love with each other, once graduation rolled around, he deployed with the army. We wrote to each other as much as we could, but when he returned, he wasn't the same man I'd fallen for. He changed; or rather, the army changed him. I was heartbroken because he turned to drinking and I couldn't stand watching him self-destruct any longer. Fast forward to three years later, he had sobered up, got clean, and was starting his own business."

"Wow…what an achievement."

"Yeah, it was. I was so proud of him, but he had moved to Florida to start his business and begged me to move so we could be together again. I was hesitant because my family was all here, and I couldn't fully trust that he wouldn't slip up and start drinking again. I let those fears smother me to the point where I backed out from moving. Although he said he understood and would wait for me to decide, by the time I finally geared up the courage to do it, he had met someone else down there." I hear her breathing softly on the other end, wondering how I never knew this about her. "What's worse is, I flew down to surprise him when I saw them together. I knew she wasn't a fling or some random girl because you could see the love they had for each other in their eyes, and that's when I knew. I was too late."

"Wow, Nora…" is all I can muster up to say.

"Fate handed me a second chance, and I didn't take it, Vada. It's something I have to live with for the rest of my life, but that doesn't mean you do."

I don't know when I started crying, but I feel tears streaming down my cheeks. I don't know why, but I just feel so sad that Nora missed out on something as wonderful as love.

"So you never met someone after him?"

"Oh, I did. I eventually tried dating other men, even married one, but I always compared them to Adam. The connection and love between us never felt as strong or authentic as the one we had. So I had failed relationships, eventually a failed marriage, and well, here I am."

"Geez, Nora. Way to hit me right in the feels." I wipe away another tear. "You know it's not too late for you," I say with a hint of seriousness.

"Oh you know I'm too set in my ways," she tells me as if I had no idea.

"Well, if you ever found Adam again and get that third chance, you best invite me to the wedding." I chuckle.

"You got it, dear."

We chat for a few more minutes before hanging up. I see Olivia's Bible organizer on the table and flip to the current month to check out the rest of the schedule. There's only a week left before the tour's over, but I don't know if I can wait that long to see him again.

I'm not going to waste our second chance.

As the Uber drives through the Charleston streets, I can't wipe the smile off my face. Olivia nearly murdered me when I told her I was leaving early. I only had one signing event left. The rest of my schedule was filled with interviews that I had her reschedule as phone interviews instead. I'd fly out for the signing this weekend, but I couldn't wait any longer to see Ethan, so I flew from Texas right to Charleston.

I decided not to tell him I'm coming so I can surprise him; however, after arriving at the house and seeing a bunch of random supplies laying around, I'm not sure if surprising him was the right way to go.

"Ethan?" I call out, watching my step as I walk through the house.

I head out back where Henry is clucking around but luckily doesn't come charging at me. Noticing the cottage door is wide open, I step closer and hear music coming from inside.

"Ethan?" I call again, but the music's too loud.

As soon as I round the doorway, I see him inside wearing tight jeans and a handyman's belt. He's shirtless, and sweat drips down his muscular back. Leaning against the doorway, I admire how fucking good he looks right now. It takes a moment for me to realize what he's doing. All the furniture is gone, the walls have been repainted, and the carpet looks like it was steam-cleaned. That's when I notice the little reading nook in the corner he's currently hammering nails into.

What in the world is he doing?

The song playing through the speakers comes to an end, and that's when I take my opportunity to let it be known I'm here.

"Knock, knock," I say loud enough for him to hear.

He spins around, and when his eyes find mine, his lips transform into the biggest smile I've ever seen.

"Holy fuck," he gasps, charging for me. Wrapping his arms around me, he pulls me up and presses a deep kiss against my lips. "What are you doing here already?"

I tighten my arms around his neck and press my mouth back on his. "I had to see you," is all the explanation I give him.

"You came back to me." He smiles, looking me over as if to make sure I'm really here.

I nod, tears stinging my eyes at the realization of how much I love this man.

"I couldn't spend another day away from you," I tell him, his arms holding me in place against his chest.

"Well, I wanted to surprise you, but..." He turns slightly, glancing around the room. "I'm building you your dream office space."

"Wait, really?" I look around and am in awe at everything he's doing. "I can't believe you'd do that for me."

"Are you kidding? This is where it all happened, baby. You touching yourself, fantasizing about me, and—"

"Oh my God, shut up!" I blush, laughing. "It is a dream though." I look around again. "You even added shelves."

"Of course!" He smiles. "I have it all designed. You're going to love it."

I kiss him—hard and without reservation.

"That's the sweetest damn thing anyone's ever done for me."

"I'd do anything for you, Vada. Anything," he whispers, pressing his forehead against mine.

"You're too good to be true," I tell him, meaning every word. "That's why I had to come back."

"What do you mean?"

"I had to tell you…" I pause briefly, getting ahold of my nerves.

"What?" He looks nervous for a split-second.

"I had to come tell you how in love with you I am, and that I'd be a fool to walk away from someone as amazing as you. I'm not running away from love this time. I want you—*forever*. I love you, Ethan Rochester."

He plants his lips back on mine, taking steps until my back hits the wall and he pins me there with his hard body.

"Fuck, Vada…I don't think those words have ever sounded so sweet till they came from your lips. I love you so goddamn much. You have no idea how happy you just made me." He presses his mouth back down on mine before I can reply, which is totally okay with me because what came next didn't need words.

EPILOGUE

ETHAN

TWO YEARS LATER...

I'M COVERED in clay and need to shower before heading in for the night, but I can't pass up the opportunity to sneak inside the nursery first.

My gorgeous wife is rocking our baby and humming as she nurses him. It's the most beautiful image in the entire world, everything I ever could've imagined. And more.

"How's it going?" I whisper, grabbing her attention as I lean against the doorway.

She smiles up at me, a noticeable glow circulating her face.

"He's just like his father. Gravitates to the left more than the right." She chuckles, holding his precious little hand.

"We Rochester men know what we like," I say with an unapologetic shrug. "Plus, the left one is bigger." I flash her a wide, knowing grin.

She rolls her eyes and looks back down at him. Pushing off the doorway, I walk over to them and press a kiss to her head.

"I still can't get over how much he looks like you," Vada says, rubbing her finger along his soft cheek.

"Yeah, but he's probably got his mama's sassy mouth."

She chuckles, softly. "And his daddy's crass attitude."

"The kid's gonna be a spitfire, no doubt." I lean down and press a soft kiss on her lips. "I'm going to hop in the shower if you want to join me after he's asleep." I flash her a wink, telling her everything I need to.

"You know we can't have sex for six weeks after giving birth," she reminds me as if I could've forgotten that little detail.

"I know, but that doesn't mean I can't feast on other parts of you," I tease.

Shaking her head at me, she bites down on her lower lip to conceal her smile. "You're bad."

"And you wrote a whole book telling everyone how much you love the bad boy, so there's no turning back now," I remind her smirking, and she wrinkles her nose at me before I lean down and kiss the top of London's head. He barely fidgets from my contact—too busy eating.

I head to the shower with a toothy grin on my face. I can't help it. I'm happier than I ever thought possible.

When we found out Vada was pregnant, I panicked at first. Although I was excited to be starting a family with her, I couldn't help that fear inside that something was going to go wrong again, and I'd lose everything all over again. I knew Vada felt it too, but we leaned on each other for love and support, which helped get through those nine months.

MY WEEK WITH THE BAD BOY

Everything went great during her pregnancy, and even her labor was smooth without any complications. The relief that struck me when he was finally here was unlike anything I'd experienced before. Just knowing I could hold him brought me on an emotional roller coaster. London was born a whopping nine pounds and a head full of dark hair. It was an indescribable feeling and one I'll never forget.

As soon as we found out we were having a boy, I was flooded with memories of Alana and Paris. I hated that I felt like I was replacing them somehow, although I knew that was far from the truth. Vada knew how important it was for me to keep their memories alive. She didn't change much in the nursery, knowing I'd want to keep certain things. She never pressed me on it, and I loved her even more for that. She wanted to keep the memories of my family alive too, and that meant more to me than anything.

I'm on cloud nine as I begin rinsing off my body in the shower and hear Vada sneaking in behind me. Spinning around, I gasp when I see her kneeling down in front of me.

"What are you—"

"Taking care of my man." She smiles up at me, grabbing ahold of my shaft as the water cascades on my back and blocking her. "Unless you'd like to jerk off in the shower alone again?" she teases, feistier than usual.

"Fuck, Vada…" I groan as she swirls her tongue around my piercing, knowing just much it turns me on. "And for the record, I don't jerk off in the shower." I pause before continuing, "*Anymore.*"

She chuckles, releasing the tip. "Yeah, okay, Casanova.

That's not what you inspired in chapter sixteen of my newest book," she reminds me with a wink.

"That was one time," I defend. "And only because you were being a cock tease."

She bursts out laughing. "I was six months pregnant and out of clothes to wear," she reminds me, and memories of her wearing my T-shirts starts getting me hot all over again.

"Yeah." I flash her a knowing smile. "You should *always* be pregnant, wearing my shirts, and *only* my shirts."

She waggles her brows as she licks the length of my shaft and begins pumping it. Fuck, she's so good at knowing exactly what I like. I wrap my hand in her hair and fist it as she works me all the way to orgasm.

Reaching down, I grab her hand and pull her up. I press my mouth against hers and kiss her until both our lips are swollen. I clean both of us, taking my time as I wash and rinse her off.

"God, you're so beautiful," I tell her along her ear as I inhale her fresh, sweet scent. "Perfect in every way."

"That's always a nice thing to hear after having baby spit-up and poop on your clothes all day," she says, choking back a laugh.

I smile, turning her around so I can look into her eyes. Cupping her cheeks, I press one more soft kiss against her lips. "I couldn't imagine life getting any better, baby. Starting a family and being truly happy is all that matters."

"Look at you, smooth talker," she teases, resting her lips against mine. "Guess my writing is starting to wear off on you."

"Oh, sweetheart," I drawl, pulling back slightly. "Gorgeous

brunettes who suck my cock like that..." I glance down, smirking, "...are my kryptonite."

"I bet they are," she says, laughing at the seriousness of my tone.

I lead her out and dry us both off. As I wrap a towel around my waist, I hear London stirring in his crib. Vada starts heading for the nursery when I stop her and pull her back.

"I'll take this shift, babe. You get some sleep." I kiss her on the cheek before walking the rest of the way to the nursery.

Before opening the door, I glance down the hall and see Oliver and Wilma snuggled up together. Oliver's licking Wilma's face, and Wilma's purring loudly.

"Get a room you two," I mock, rolling my eyes at how much they love each other. Once Vada confirmed she was moving in, we flew up to Chicago together so I could help her pack and arrange for all her things to get shipped down here. Oliver didn't exactly warm up to me right away, which caused concern on how he'd react to Wilma.

Suffice it to say, he warmed up to Wilma much sooner.

After meeting Nora though, I could see why Oliver was hesitant about meeting new people. He was used to being around strong, hard-headed women and saw me as a threat. Eventually, we had a heart-to-heart and agreed to both be the men of the house.

Walking into the nursery, I peek in the crib and see London's fussing and unraveling from his swaddle. I pick him up, check his diaper, and wrap him back up in his blanket before seating us in the rocking chair.

"Listen, little guy," I begin, brushing my finger softly along his face. "Your mama hasn't slept in five weeks, and I'm going to need her to be as refreshed as possible in about the next week or so, which means you have to start sleeping for a few hours at a time. Now, I'm not above bribery and negotiations, so you just tell me what you want. A playset? Jordan High-tops? A Mustang when you turn sixteen? I mean, you name it, and I'll make it happen, okay? As long as you give me one hour alone with your mama. Well, let's just say two." I smile as he eyes me curiously as if I've lost my mind. "Do we have a deal?"

I press my finger to his little palm and high-five him.

"If I didn't think that was the cutest thing I ever saw, I'd call you pathetic for trying to bribe our newborn baby so we can have sex." Vada leans against the doorway, shaking her head at me and smiling.

"Not just any sex, though," I defend, and her smile widens. "Postpartum sex, which means as soon as the doctor gives the thumbs up, I'm stripping off all your clothes."

"We're not having sex in the doctor's office!" she warns.

"Babe…" I tease. "Never say never."

She rolls her eyes and shakes her head.

"C'mon. Think of all the good book inspiration." I grin.

"You're horrible," she quips. She walks over to us and presses a gentle kiss on London's head. "Your daddy is bad, London. Such a *bad boy*."

"Yes, but a good, bad boy," I correct with a smile.

"For now." She winks.

After getting London back to sleep and in his crib, Vada and I head into our room. "Are you writing tonight?" I ask, knowing she's been gradually getting back to it.

"I think so. Olivia's been sending me some juicy details," she explains with a knowing grin.

"Really?"

"Yup. Apparently, the new author she's assisting is forcing her to road trip with a new cover model to a signing event across the country."

"Oh yeah? Is he a bad boy, too?" I wink.

"According to Olivia, he's worse."

"Worse? How?"

"He has quite the reputation of being a *fuck boy* and Olivia isn't happy about it."

I laugh. "I give them a week, and they'll be doing it."

She winces. "Ethan!"

Chuckling, I shrug. "What? You know that's *exactly* what's going to happen."

"Well, in my book, of course. But Olivia is a bit uptight," she reminds me. "She's not one to sleep around." She told me all about Olivia when she worked for her before moving here.

I smirk at my internal prediction. "Then I guess he'll have fun breaking her in."

Coming Next

My Week

WITH THE F*ck Boy

USA TODAY BESTSELLING AUTHOR

BROOKE CUMBERLAND
AND LYRA PARISH

Coming Spring 2018

MY WEEK WITH THE FUCK BOY BLURB

Never trust a man who gets paid to take off his clothes for a living and then uses it as a pick-up line to get girls in bed with him.

That should've been enough for me to call in sick that day.

I've worked with male cover models like him before and they're all the same—smooth-talking, sexy-as-sin, egotistical know-it-alls who think they're God's gift to women—all traits I know to steer clear of.

Assisting authors comes with many perks—reading on the job, using my organizing skills on a daily basis, drinking coffee by the gallons—but Maverick Kingston barges into my life and demands more than I can handle.

When we're forced to road trip across the country together, he pushes every boundary I have and rearranges my thoughts on *playing it safe*. And when he "accidentally" drops his towel, he makes it very clear what he's offering and proves he's packing more than abs of steel under his clothes.

Being a personal assistant has one golden rule—never mix business with pleasure. But you know what they say about rules? *F*ck 'em.*

Connect with us:

FIND ALL OUR CURRENT UPDATES & ONLINE SHOP HERE:
www.brookeandlyrabooks.com

SUBSCRIBE TO OUR MONTHLY NEWSLETTER:
brookeandlyrabooks.com/newsletter

Brooke and Lyra also write under the duo pseudonym,
Kennedy Fox. You can find all their titles and updates here:
www.kennedyfoxbooks.com

About the Author

Brooke Cumberland is a *USA Today* Bestselling author who wears many hats on any given day. She also co-writes under the *USA Today* bestselling duo pseudonym, Kennedy Fox with her literary soul mate, Lyra Parish. She lives in the frozen tundra of Packer Nation with her husband, 7-year-old wild child, and two teenage stepsons. When she's not writing, you can find her reading, listening to music, and spending time with her family. Brooke's addicted to coffee, leggings, & naps. She found her passion for telling stories during winter break one year in grad school—and she hasn't stopped since.

Connect with Brooke:

Website:
www.brookecumberland.com

Facebook Page:
Facebook.com/authorbrookecumberland

Facebook Reader Group:
Facebook.com/groups/brookecumberlandsbookies

Follow on Instagram:
Instagram.com/brookecumberland_xo

Follow on Book Bub:
Bookbub.com/authors/brooke-cumberland

Follow on Amazon/Find all her titles here:
amazon.com/author/brookecumberland

Subscribe to monthly newsletter:
brookecumberland.com/newsletter

Books by Brooke:

The Riverside Trilogy
Kitchen Affairs
Kitchen Scandals
Kitchen Promises

The Spark Series
Spark
Burn
Flame

The Intern Serials
Vols. 1-3
After the Internship

Standalone Novels
Bad Girlfriend
Dangerous Temptations
Pushing the Limits

My Week Series
My Week with the Bad Boy
My Week with the F*ck Boy
My Week with the Play Boy

About the Author

Lyra Parish loves to write, glamp, and sing obnoxiously loud at the top of her lungs in the shower. Sweet love stories (along with the dirty ones) make her gush. She is a firm believer that a person can never have too many cups of coffee, cats, or happily ever afters. When she isn't busy writing with Brooke as Kennedy Fox, she can be found sipping various beverages from her non-alcoholic drink buffet, pimp slapping excel spreadsheets, or riding her bike. Lyra lives in Texas with her glassblowing, guitar-playing hubby and black cat named, Nibbler.

Connect with Lyra:

Website:
www.lyraparish.com

Facebook Page:
Facebook.com/lyraparishauthor

Facebook Reader Group:
Facebook.com/groups/lyraparishstreetteam

Follow on Instagram:
Instagram.com/lyraparish

Follow on Book Bub:
Bookbub.com/authors/lyra-parish

Follow on Amazon/Find all her titles here:
amazon.com/author/lyraparish

Subscribe to newsletter:
lyraparish.com/newsletter

Books by Lyra:

Weakness Trilogy
Weak for Him
Weak without Him
No Longer Weak

Single Serials
Vols. 1-3

Standalone Novels
Eluded
Ace: A Band of Brothers Novel

My Week Series
My Week with the Bad Boy
My Week with the F*ck Boy
My Week with the Play Boy

CHECKMATE: THIS IS WAR

Start the Checkmate Duet Series absolutely FREE right now!
Available on all retailers - find all the buy links at
kennedyfoxbooks.com/this-is-war

Acknowledgements

Three years ago, I had a vision for a story called, My Week with the Bad Boy. It was 100% different from the plot of this story, but it's been on my mind during all the other stories I've written. Finally, I decided it was time to pour this story out of my head. It went through various plot changes and finally, I turned to Lyra and said, "You have to write this book with me. You're half my brain now and apparently I can't function without you." Of course, she was totally on board! (Because she's literally the best writing parter and friend in the world)! Though we had a packed writing schedule with our Kennedy Fox titles, we busted ass and plotted this new storyline, while keeping my original concept. It wasn't completely different from our Checkmate Duet Series world, but it was with brand new characters, and I worried how that would affect our creativeness so close to ending a six-book series. But suffice to say, we dove head first into this new world and we are so excited to bring our readers the new world of the *My Week* series! We hope you'll continue to read about all our bad boys!
-Brooke

~

Thank you to everyone who's supported us over the past five

years as we navigate our writing journeys. It's not been easy, but it's been fun, and no one can ever take that away from us.

We've worked with some amazing people over the years. This past year has been life-changing and we'll never forget everyone who's always been there for us.

Thank you to our team—Golden (FuriousFotog) and Joey Berry for giving us the PERFECT image as Ethan! Mitzi and Virginia for polishing our words just right! Letitia (RBA Designs) for being a kick-ass designer and seeing our vision even when we don't. Our PR and blogger team! We couldn't do this without y'all!

We have an amazing bookstagram team as well and we have had the best time meeting new readers and bloggers. Thank you from the bottom of our hearts for being so loyal and supportive!

To our beta team, thank you for expressing all your feelings and reactions with GIFs as you read MWwtBB and helping us feel confident in our work!

To all our readers, new and old—THANK YOU! You're the reason we get to continue pursuing our passion every single day!

And of course, a huge thank you to our families. There's no manual for being married to a writer (although, there really should be) and you put up with so much. Your support and love help us get through the long hours, late nights, and zombie-like behavior. Writing is the BEST job in the world and you help us make it possible.

-Brooke & Lyra
www.brookeandlyrabooks.com

83056015R00157

Made in the USA
Columbia, SC
22 December 2017